SA/Am

D0872731

DISCARD

| DATE DUE | | |
|---|---|---|
| JAN 0 2 2019 | | |
| NOV 2 9 2019 | | |
| | | |
| | | |
| | | |
| | | |
| | | |
| | | |
| | | |
| | | |
| | | |

3YZJR000274881
Ione, Larissa        37310
Razr
AF ION            $9.99

SCF

Antlers Public Library
104 S.E. 2nd Street
Antlers, OK  74523

# Razr

# Also from Larissa Ione

# Razr

## A Demonica Underworld Novella

# By Larissa Ione

1001 Dark Nights

EVIL EYE
CONCEPTS

Razr
A Demonica Underworld Novella
By Larissa Ione

1001 Dark Nights

Copyright 2017 Larissa Ione
ISBN: 978-1-945920-21-9

Forward: Copyright 2014 M. J. Rose

Published by Evil Eye Concepts, Incorporated

All rights reserved. No part of this book may be reproduced, scanned, or distributed in any printed or electronic form without permission. Please do not participate in or encourage piracy of copyrighted materials in violation of the author's rights.

This is a work of fiction. Names, places, characters and incidents are the product of the author's imagination and are fictitious. Any resemblance to actual persons, living or dead, events or establishments is solely coincidental.

# Acknowledgments from the Author

I just want to send a million thank-you's to the entire Evil Eye team. You are like family to me, and I love you dearly! I can't wait to see you all next time!

And to my readers, I just want to thank you for sticking with me on this journey. I promise you, it's just getting started and there is a LOT more to come...

Sign up for the 1001 Dark Nights Newsletter
and be entered to win a Tiffany Key necklace.

There's a contest every month!

Go to www.1001DarkNights.com to subscribe.

As a bonus, all subscribers will receive a free
1001 Dark Nights story
*The First Night*
by Lexi Blake & M.J. Rose

# One Thousand and One Dark Nights

*Once upon a time, in the future…*

*I was a student fascinated with stories and learning.
I studied philosophy, poetry, history, the occult, and
the art and science of love and magic. I had a vast
library at my father's home and collected thousands
of volumes of fantastic tales.*

*I learned all about ancient races and bygone
times. About myths and legends and dreams of all
people through the millennium. And the more I read
the stronger my imagination grew until I discovered
that I was able to travel into the stories... to actually
become part of them.*

*I wish I could say that I listened to my teacher
and respected my gift, as I ought to have. If I had, I
would not be telling you this tale now.
But I was foolhardy and confused, showing off
with bravery.*

*One afternoon, curious about the myth of the
Arabian Nights, I traveled back to ancient Persia to
see for myself if it was true that every day Shahryar
(Persian: شهریار, "king") married a new virgin, and then
sent yesterday's wife to be beheaded. It was written
and I had read, that by the time he met Scheherazade,
the vizier's daughter, he'd killed one thousand
women.*

*Something went wrong with my efforts. I arrived in the midst of the story and somehow exchanged places with Scheherazade – a phenomena that had never occurred before and that still to this day, I cannot explain.*

*Now I am trapped in that ancient past. I have taken on Scheherazade's life and the only way I can protect myself and stay alive is to do what she did to protect herself and stay alive.*

*Every night the King calls for me and listens as I spin tales. And when the evening ends and dawn breaks, I stop at a point that leaves him breathless and yearning for more. And so the King spares my life for one more day, so that he might hear the rest of my dark tale.*

*As soon as I finish a story... I begin a new one... like the one that you, dear reader, have before you now.*

# Glossary

*Faeway*—Mystical "hotspots" in the human realm that elves can use to travel to and from their home realm.

*Fallen Angel*--Believed to be evil by most humans, fallen angels can be grouped into two categories: True Fallen and Unfallen. Unfallen angels have been cast from Heaven and are earthbound, living a life in which they are neither truly good nor truly evil. In this state, they can, rarely, earn their way back into Heaven. Or they can choose to enter Sheoul, the demon realm, in order to complete their fall and become True Fallens.

*Harrowgate*--Vertical portals, invisible to humans, used to travel between locations on Earth and Sheoul. A very few beings can summon their own personal Harrowgates.

*Inner Sanctum*—A realm within Sheoul-gra that consists of five Rings, each housing the souls of demons categorized by their level of evil as defined by the Ufelskala. The Inner Sanctum is run by the fallen angel Hades and his staff of wardens, all fallen angels. Access to the Inner Sanctum is strictly limited, as the demons imprisoned within can take advantage of any outside object or living person in order to escape.

*Memitim*—Sired exclusively by Azagoth, Memitim are earthbound angels assigned to protect important humans called Primori. Memitim remain earthbound until they complete their duties, at which time they Ascend, earning their wings and entry into Heaven.

*Primori*—Humans and demons whose lives are fated to affect the world in some crucial way.

*Sheoul*--Demon realm some call Hell. Located on its own plane deep in the bowels of the Earth, accessible to most only by Harrowgates and hellmouths.

*Sheoul-gra*--A realm that exists independently of Sheoul, it is overseen by Azagoth, also known as the Grim Reaper. Within Sheoul-gra is the Inner Sanctum, where demon souls go to be kept in torturous limbo until they can be reborn.

*Ufelskala*—A scoring system for demons, based on their degree of evil. All supernatural creatures and evil humans can be categorized into the five Tiers, with the Fifth Tier comprising of the worst of the wicked.

# Chapter One

Inside the confines of his boss's office, demons swirled in the air all around Razr. The screaming, tortured souls begged for mercy or shouted obscenities and threats.

Razr tapped the ring on his right index finger against his thigh as Azagoth, an ancient being also known as the Grim Reaper, sent tiny bursts of power at each one, making them screech in agony.

Azagoth was playing with them, toying with them the way a cat would a mouse. His plush office, deep inside the underworld realm known as Sheoul-gra, had turned into a grim playground of pain.

Pain was something Razr could deal with. Subservience was not, and after hundreds of years spent as an elite battle angel, being sentenced to serve Azagoth was humiliating as shit. But it was Razr's own fault, and ultimately, he was lucky. After all, he'd been kicked out of Heaven, but he hadn't lost his wings.

No, his angelic wings and their fate would be determined by whether or not he could repair the damage he'd done a century ago.

So, yeah. Hanging out with Azagoth and his band of freaky minions wasn't exactly a great gig, but it could be worse. Still, as he stood across from Azagoth, who looked especially Grim Reaper-y in a black hooded robe, his green eyes glowing from the shadows, Razr didn't see how it could be worse at this particular moment.

Azagoth flicked his hand in dismissal, and a wave of *griminions* swarmed into the room like ants, their own miniature black robes dragging on the floor, their faces hidden by cowls. They gathered the demon souls and scurried away, disappearing into a tunnel in the wall to whatever hellhole they belonged in. When Azagoth turned his attention to Razr, the chill that settled on Razr's skin quickly penetrated all the way to his bones.

"I want to know why you wear a damned burlap sack and flip-flops every damned day. You have access to anything you want, but the only times you aren't dressed like a medieval monk are when you leave Sheoul-gra." Azagoth cocked his head and intensified his focus, leaving Razr feeling like a germ under a microscope. "Is the clothing part of your punishment?"

Razr started. He'd been living in Sheoul-gra and working in Azagoth's employ for over a year now, and this was the first time his boss had asked him anything that wasn't work-related.

"Yes," Razr said, but it was a simple answer to a complex issue.

"Your situation is unique. You aren't fallen, but you aren't a Heavenly angel, either. You aren't even Unfallen," Azagoth said, referring to the in-between state of an angel who had lost his wings but who hadn't entered Sheoul, the demon realm, to complete his fall from grace. He glided over to the wet bar and splashed rum into two glasses. "Heaven created a new designation of angel just for you."

"Yeah," Razr drawled. "Ain't I special." Except he wasn't. There was another who had shared his status, his former lover Darlah, presumed dead after failing to return from a mission.

A mission that was now Razr's alone.

Azagoth handed him one of the glasses, and Razr struggled to hide his surprise. And suspicion. The other male rarely acknowledged his existence, let alone treated him like an equal. "For some reason, you *are* special."

This was really getting weird. Azagoth had never shown any interest in him, but honestly, Razr was shocked that the guy didn't know more about Razr's story. He'd figured Heaven would have given Azagoth the full scoop, but apparently not.

"What I can't figure out," Azagoth continued, "is why you haven't managed to take care of your business and get back into Heaven."

Unable to remain still under this bizarre scrutiny, Razr swirled the rum around in his glass. "It's not like you give me a lot of free time."

"So it's my fault?" Azagoth's voice was smooth as velvet and just dark enough to raise the hair on Razr's head. One didn't just accuse the Grim Reaper of stalling shit. Not if they liked wearing their skin.

"Not at all," Razr replied carefully, because his skin was pretty useful right where it was. "It's just that I have limited resources in Sheoul-gra. I need more time in the human and demon realms."

Instead, he was stuck training Azagoth's army of Memitim and the Unfallen refugees who had taken sanctuary here. Although, in truth, if Razr *had* to work for Azagoth, schooling angels on battle tactics wasn't the suckiest thing he could do. It was a challenge he enjoyed, given that angels were notoriously hard to get to work together, and his specialty was teamwork.

He'd just rather be training angels in Heaven than in Hell.

The door to the office opened, and Zhubaal, Azagoth's right-hand man and Razr's direct superior, escorted a broad-shouldered male who smelled of sunshine inside. The angel, a big bastard in a plain brown hooded robe who went by the code name of Jim Bob, strode past Azagoth and stopped in front of Razr, which was odd, considering the angel tended to keep conversation limited to Azagoth.

Which probably meant he wasn't being straight with his fellow angels about his business here. Razr had never met the guy in Heaven, so he had no idea of Jim Bob's real name or what his game was, but if Razr was ever reinstated as a full angel, he'd have to do some investigating.

"What happened to your head?"

Razr jammed his fingers through his short, dark hair. "What, you liked the bald look better?"

"Yes. Also, this is for you." He held out a thick gold business card embossed with silver letters that spelled out "The Wardens."

"What is it?"

"It's where you'll find what you're looking for."

Razr stopped breathing even as his heart revved from a sudden injection of hope-fueled adrenaline. He stared at the silver letters as if they were a lifeline and he was drowning. "Are...are you sure?"

"I have it on good authority."

Razr's hand shook so hard he nearly dropped the card. This was it. The way to repair some, if not all, of the damage he and his teammates caused when they'd lost three of Heaven's most valuable weapons, the Gems of Enoch, and got their human custodians killed. One gem, the Terra Amethyst, had been recovered, but two remained: Darlah's Fire Garnet and Razr's Ice Diamond.

Finding either or both would return Razr to full angel status and erase the stain on his reputation...and his soul.

Azagoth, clearly knowing what Razr was thinking, nodded. "Go," he said. "Take as much time as you need."

Razr sucked in a stunned breath, but really, he shouldn't be all that shocked. Azagoth might have a reputation for cruelty, but he was generous with those who were loyal to him. Razr was about to thank him when the angel wing glyph on the back of his hand, usually invisible, began to glow. Fuck. It had been less than twenty-four hours since the last time. He usually got thirty-six, give or take a couple of hours, to recover. Although once he'd gone barely eight. The random nature of this particular angelic punishment was a pain in the ass.

"That was shitty timing." Azagoth, the King of Demon Souls and Understatements, pulled a well-worn cat-o'-nines out of his desk drawer. Because, of course, one must always be prepared for spur-of-the-moment torture. He held up the weapon with way too much enthusiasm. "Mine or yours?"

Razr's personal flogger was in his pocket, and he swore he felt it burning through his robes. "Yours," he muttered, figuring it was always better to get someone else's stuff bloody.

Azagoth held the cat out to Jim Bob. "Want the honor?"

Razr bit back a groan as the angel took the weapon and stroked it like an old lover. "It's been a long time."

"Really?" Razr said. "Because you seem like the type who gets off on torture." It was a stupid thing to say to someone who was far more powerful and who was about to turn Razr's back into hamburger, but he'd never been known for his tact.

Jim Bob, who rarely even smiled, laughed. Clearly, the guy's sense of humor circled the gallows. Razr would respect that if he weren't the one swinging at the end of the rope. "Will you stand or kneel?"

"Well," he drawled as he dropped his robe so he was standing naked in front of Azagoth, Jim Bob, and Zhubaal, "I figure I'll start on my feet and end on my knees. That's usually how it goes."

Jim Bob made a "turn-around" gesture, and after taking a deep, steadying breath, Razr assumed the position, bracing himself against the wall with his palms. "How many?"

"Six," Azagoth said before Razr could answer. "I don't know why."

"I do." Jim Bob's soft reply hung in the air and reeled through Razr's mind. How did Jim Bob know? Sure, everyone in Heaven probably knew about Razr's screw-up with the Gems of Enoch, but few were privy to the specifics of his punishment. The guy must be well connected in Heaven, which only added to the mystery of his dealings with Azagoth.

The whistle of the nine leather straps, each tipped by sharp bone spurs singing through the air, interrupted Razr's thoughts. Pain exploded across his shoulder blades and forced a grunt from him. But not a scream. He never screamed.

The second blow was worse, the third so intense that he sagged to his knees. Usually he could stay on his feet until the fifth strike, but Jim Bob was strong, and he wasn't holding back. That was the thing about floggings in the angel and demon worlds versus the human one; Razr could take hundreds of lashings from a human. Hell, he could take thousands and not die.

But when someone with superior strength and mystical capabilities was wielding the whip, the damage increased by a factor of *holy shit*.

The fourth blow knocked the breath from his lungs, and the fifth made him see stars.

The sixth, placed low on his hips, knocked him onto the cold floor, sprawled in a pool of his own blood.

Maybe this was the last time. *Please let this be the last time*, he thought, just before he passed out.

# Chapter Two

"Ma'am, pardon my French, but you're full of shit. There are no fucking deposits here. No Taaffeite has ever been found in Madagascar. This is a waste of time and a waste of a fuckton of money. I don't care about your credentials. Like I said, you're full of shit."

Jedda Brighton resisted the urge to punch the man in his unshaven, saggy face the way she'd been wanting to do for the last two weeks. Two weeks of putting up with the mining engineer's alcohol-fueled crude talk and casual sexism, which he blew off as her being an oversensitive snowflake when she called him on it. Two weeks of watching him treat the local diggers like slaves. Two weeks of listening to him bitch about his "whore of an ex-wife" and "outrageous" child support. He was the type of asshole who, if a woman turned down his advances, would accuse her of being a lesbian.

Because sure, didn't all women love an overweight, abusive slob who looked and smelled like a walking hangover and who thought he was God's gift to women? If not for his considerable wealth, no woman would put up with him, and he either didn't know that, or he didn't care, which made him either stupid, or scum, or both.

Jedda was going to go with both. Hell, she wouldn't put up with him for even this job if it weren't for the fact that she needed him to dig for gems she couldn't otherwise reach on her own.

"First of all," she said in her snootiest voice, "I'm fluent in a dozen languages, including French, and what you just said wasn't even close. Second, I'm the best damned gemologist *and* mineralogist in the world, and if I say there's a bloody fortune in Taaffeite here, you can rest assured that there is." She smiled sweetly. "And after you find it, you can shove it up your ass."

He waggled sandy brows that glistened with sweat from the oppressive heat in this godforsaken jungle. "How about you do it for me?"

Sweet Satie One-Eye, he was disgusting, and even Satie, an elf hero of lore who had fought giant demonic maggots, would agree. This guy was a whisky dick personified. Adjusting her hard hat, Jedda stepped around him and headed inside the mine. "You really don't want to taunt me."

"Taunt...or tempt?"

Ugh. Gross. In the last two weeks, had this idiot not figured out that she didn't play well with others? Especially not *human* others? She supposed she should at least be grateful he wasn't aware that she wasn't human, but then, maybe if he knew she was an immortal being he'd leave her alone.

She might have to reveal her secret just to freak him out.

He followed her down the relatively cool shaft, past workers who were busy extracting gemstones that, while less valuable than Taaffeite, would still net Tom's mining company a nice profit. But he still played the injured party, insisting that this venture was a waste of time and resources.

She knew better. As a gem elf, she could sense minerals that gave off energy undetectable to humans, energy that she survived on. Enchanted stones, gems that had been blessed or cursed or used in powerful rituals, were the most life-enhancing, especially when absorbed into a gem elf's body, but there was always a risk involved when using them, as she knew very well.

Her boots crunched down on uneven ground, but she kept her footing, her enhanced reflexes and night vision giving her a distinct advantage over humans and most demons. Tom followed her much more slowly, cursing now and then, muttering his displeasure at being bested by a woman. She had no doubt he was generally capable in situations like this as long as he kept to a safe human pace, but his macho attitude wouldn't let him lag behind, and he had no idea she was genetically suited for this exact situation.

She laughed when she heard him trip and fall. "You okay?" she called back. "I can slow down if you need me to."

"I'm fine," he barked, and she laughed again at his volley of obscenities. What an asshole.

She kept going, reaching out with her senses as she navigated the dark tunnels. She could feel the elemental vibrations change as she passed each new mineral, some of them leaving no more impression on her than common gravel, others whispering to her like potential lovers. But none of them possessed the special signature of the Taaffeite. Still, she was close. She couldn't quite feel the deposit yet, but she could smell it, a faint anise and berry tang in the musty earth that made her mouth water. Every gemstone had its own unique scent, some spicy, some sweet, and Taaffeite was a delectable combination of both.

What felt like a cool breeze tickled her skin from an unexplored tunnel on the right. It was narrow, with jagged stones jutting from the sides like a giant cheese grater. Carefully, she went to her hands and knees and started to crawl.

"Hold up there, sweetheart," Tom called out. "My men haven't reinforced this yet, and I'm not about to—"

"Shut up!" She paused, inhaled, tasting the sharp bite of beryllium and aluminum on the back of her tongue. "It's here," she breathed excitedly.

Giddy with anticipation, she turned up the intensity of the light on her helmet, and there, just ahead in a space big enough to stand, was a glint of violet peeking out of the boring gray and brown stone all around it.

Grinning, she scrambled the remaining distance in the crawlspace, and when she stood, she marveled at the sight of a thick vein of one of the rarest gemstones in the world. There was another vein near the ceiling, and she could sense more deep in the walls. She doubted there was more than about seven hundred carats' worth of Taaffeite here, but at around three to four thousand dollars per carat on the human market and double that on the demon one, the stones would net a respectable haul. And because it was so rare, adding even a hundred carats to the market would increase the value and the demand since right now few knew about it, and those who did were collectors.

Very carefully, she plucked a chisel from her gear belt and dug a jagged hunk of stone from the surrounding rock. Under the light from her helmet, the purple gem glittered, even with all the rough material coating it. Its aura glowed with stunning intensity, something the obnoxious human crawling toward her wouldn't be able to see.

She closed her fist around the gem and inhaled, letting its vibrations absorb into her body. Power pounded through her, making her flesh throb and her blood surge. This was a natural stone, untouched by anyone, so its energy was pure, neutral, and unenhanced. It would give her added strength and stamina, but it wouldn't add or subtract from any of her special abilities.

It was, in the simplest of terms, life.

Tom emerged from the tunnel like a grumpy bear awakened from hibernation. "What are you doing?" As he stood, dirt cascaded off him in a choking cloud of dust.

She opened her fist. The gem was gone, the earth and rock that had surrounded it nothing but crumbs in her palm. "I'm admiring my find," she said, letting the remains fall to the floor of the cave.

As he studied a vein of Taaffeite, she dug another, about the size of her thumb, from a crevice nearby.

"Nice work, honey," he said, talking directly at her breasts. "I'm impressed. Everyone said you're the best. Should have listened."

"Yes, you should have." She turned toward the tunnel to escape this cretin, and as she did, he slapped her on the ass. Instant, searing rage welled in her chest, and fuck it, she was done with his shit. Her anger destroyed the tight control she kept on herself, and suddenly the cave lit up with the soft, iridescent glow emanating from her skin. She knew her eyes, normally ice blue, were glowing as well, still blue, but more intense.

"What the fuck?" Tom leaped backward in fear, but the fear turned to terror when she smiled and held up the gem she'd just dug out of the earth.

"Remember what I said you could do with the Taaffeite when we found it?"

Later, she wondered if the other miners heard his shouts for help. She also wondered how long it had taken for that stone to dislodge itself from his ass—and if he'd sifted through his shit to find it.

# Chapter Three

Razr had always liked Scotland. The weather was moody, the landscape could almost be described as arrogant, and the people were tough as shit. Liking the place was a crazy contradiction for him, because he both envied the humans who lived here and was thankful he didn't *have* to live here. Nice place to visit, and all that.

Today's visit, however, wasn't about seeing the sights, drinking the whisky, or eating haggis. Just twenty-four hours after Jim Bob gave him the gold card, Razr was taking back what was his and restoring his dignity and reputation.

Since he'd lost his ability to flash from place to place when his wings were bound, he'd taken a Harrowgate, a transportation system used by demons to travel around the human and demon realms, to the outskirts of a walled village populated by dhampires. Few knew of the existence of the half-vampire, half-werewolf beings, and even fewer knew about their Scottish villages. Humans were especially clueless; their eyes might see the towns and the people, but their primitive minds wouldn't register any of it, and wards placed around the properties would repel humans on a subconscious level.

His boots left deep prints in the soggy earth and fog dampened his jeans and formed tiny droplets on his jacket as he walked toward the village's walled east entrance. He could smell the recent rain and taste the ocean salt in the air, but he didn't let any of that distract him from the fact that he felt more than one set of eyes keeping track of him. Dhampires were cautious folk, secretive to the point of paranoia, as vicious as vampires and as unpredictable as werewolves.

They'd gotten the best and worst of both species, and only a fool would let their guard down around them.

Just inside the village wall he was met by thatch-roofed houses and a burly female with short-cropped dark hair, razor-sharp fangs, and a crossbow slung over her shoulder. An unusual ripple of energy surrounded her, unusual in that while dhampires were certainly a formidable species, they weren't generally associated with special gifts. This dhampire, however, looked like she kicked ass with special abilities on a daily basis, and maybe bragged about it.

As a battle angel, he could appreciate that.

She propped her fists on her hips and blocked his path. He *didn't* appreciate that. "State yer business, yer species, and yer name," she said in a thick Scottish accent. "And make it quick. I don't have all day." She snapped her fingers in a show of impatience.

Man, he wished he still had angel status and more powers than the few weak defensive skills he'd been left with, because no one spoke to angels with so much disrespect. So instead of a display of power and wings, he decided to mess with her.

"Maybe I'm a human traveler named George who just wants to stop for a meal."

"Ye came through the Harrowgate, so ye aren't human or ye'd be dead, ye lyin' ballbag." She crossed her arms over her chest and leaned in. "I'll ask one more time. Who are ye, and—"

"My name is Razr," he ground out, extending the gold card Jim Bob had given him. "I'm a fallen angel, and I'd appreciate it if you got out of my face."

She sniffed and wrinkled her nose. "Ye don't smell like a fallen angel."

That was because this lyin' ballbag wasn't one. "What do fallen angels smell like?"

"Shit."

Ah. "Well, I'm newly fallen. Maybe I have to earn my stench."

Unamused, she snatched the card away and frowned down at it. "Why do ye want to see them?"

Did she think he was born yesterday? Or even a century ago? "I'm sure those who wish to see a secretive group of people don't tell you why they're here."

"No, they don't. But what they don't say is as important as what they do."

"And what am I not saying?"

She smiled, her lips peeling back from those wicked-looking fangs. "That ye're seeking something. And it's important. Which means ye need to be nice to me or ye won't get it."

Damn, he hated inferior beings on power trips. "Fine," he sighed. "You're a...sturdy female with big muscles and a voice so deep and breathy that Darth Vader would be jealous. Is that nice enough?"

She laughed, breaking the ice. "Come on." She led him down a cobblestone street lined with small houses and quaint shops, and then onto a dirt path through a thick copse of trees. He followed her until they came to a clearing, in the middle of which a stone tower stood. As they approached, a big male and a petite female exited.

A wave of power rolled off them, the same as the female who'd brought him here. And then he knew. These were the Wardens, the Triad, three dhampires chosen by fate or blood or some mystical crap to guard the most priceless things in the world. And they were in possession of his gemstone.

The male, his dark hair swinging around his shoulders, spoke first. "I'm Galen. You've already met Rhona." He gestured to the petite, fire-haired female who hung back but who radiated more power than the other two combined. "That is Isla. State your business."

"You people aren't real friendly, are you?" They stared, and he resisted the urge to taunt them more. As an angel, he was used to the stick-up-the-ass types, and he knew they often had short fuses, and he didn't want to fuck this up. "I'm here because I believe you're in possession of something that belongs to me." He held out his hand so they could see his ring. The ice-blue diamond glittered in the hazy sunlight that managed to punch through the gray sheet of clouds above. "It's this stone's larger mate."

Isla started to reach for it but pulled back at the last second. "May I?"

"You can touch the ring, but I can't remove it." No, the only way this particular piece of jewelry could come off his finger was if he was dead or his finger was severed.

She smoothed her finger over the stone. "Yes," she murmured.

"We do have its mate."

Excitement shot through him. Excitement, and a whole lot of hope. He'd been waiting decades for this moment. *Get ready, Heaven, because I'm coming home.* "Then I can have it?"

The three Wardens glanced at each other, and then, in a coordinated move, they formed a circle around him, each about ten feet away. Beneath him the ground began to glow with an eerie green light and the ice-blue gemstone he'd been hunting for a century appeared before him out of thin air.

It was as beautiful as he remembered, its oval shape and smooth, polished surface reflecting light and unpredictable angles onto the grass.

"You can hold it," Galen said, "but it cannot leave this circle."

Too relieved and enthralled to question Galen's words, Razr reached for the apple-sized diamond. The moment he came into contact with it, a sense of comfort washed over him. Comfort and joy and vindication. He wished he could have punished the evil bastards who had stolen it and the two other Gems of Enoch and murdered their hosts, but there would be time to hunt them down later. Right now he had to take his prize to his superiors and get his wings and powers unbound. After that, he could bond the gem to another human host and then finally, *finally*, he'd have access to its powers again.

But wait... Had Galen said the stone couldn't leave the circle?

Dropping his hand, he rounded on the Warden. "This diamond belongs to me. I have the right to take it."

Isla laughed, and he swore she'd just gotten taller. No, she *had* gotten taller. She now stood half a head above Galen who, at around six-five, was as tall as Razr. "We are bound by laws you can't even begin to understand, *fallen*." The emphasis she'd put on "fallen" made him wonder if she meant it as an insult...or if she knew he was lying. "You might be the original owner, but we made the storage contract with the one who gave it into our care. It is not our place to hand it over to you."

Son of a bitch. He ground his molars in frustration. His stolen property was right in front of him. His waking nightmare was within inches of being over. And these museum guards were going to keep it from happening. For the millionth time, he wished he had the full use of his powers. He couldn't even channel the gem's powers without a host to amplify its energy.

But he did have friends. Friends in very low places…and friends in very high places. If he took his case to the angelic court, they could grant him an army of angels to help him reclaim his property—which was really Heaven's property. These dhampires wouldn't stand a chance.

"I can come back with a hundred angels," he warned. "A thousand. You can't keep what is rightfully mine."

Galen barked out a laugh. "A million. It wouldn't matter. As Isla said, we're bound by laws beyond your ken. The things we store are beyond your reach. But you are welcome to try. We haven't seen much battle recently."

"Or ye could stop being a fucking dobber and find the current owner yer own damned self," Rhona suggested. "Everything ye need to know is at the tip of yer fingers."

Could it be so easy? Hastily, he palmed the diamond and closed his eyes. In a flash of light, an image popped into his mind. A female. A stunning female with long silver-blue hair and eyes the color of the stone in his hand. Her pale skin was flawless and brilliant, as if she'd walked through a cloud of diamond dust. More information came at him like a data download, and within seconds he knew where she worked and where she lived.

Smiling, he opened his eyes. And then he casually tried to pocket his diamond and walk away. The Wardens even let him.

Probably because the moment he stepped outside the glowing circle, the stone melted away and he was struck by a bolt of lightning.

Still, electrocution and third-degree burns aside, it had been a pretty good day.

# Chapter Four

It turned out that Jedda Brighton had some damned impressive credentials in the fields of gemology and mineralogy. According to Razr's cursory research on the wealthy recluse, she'd gone to the best schools, she owned her own business in the form of an outlandishly upscale London jewelry store that dealt exclusively in rare and exotic gemstones, and she was world-renowned for her uncanny ability to locate pockets of valuable minerals deep in the earth.

All of that information was public knowledge. What wasn't public knowledge—at least, human public knowledge—was that her jewelry store was a front for the underworld dealing of cursed and enchanted gems.

Which meant that she was, almost certainly, a demon.

Maybe even one of the very demons responsible for the Enoch gems' loss.

A deep growl rumbled in his chest as he made his way across the floor of the building where he expected to find his target. Mozart filled the air, lending a bizarre normalcy to the attending crowd of assorted demons, werewolves, vampires, and even a few humans who reeked of evil or greed. The massive castle, high in the mountains of Austria, was apparently the setting for this year's annual Underworld Sorcery Event, at which Jedda had been advertised as a guest speaker.

Razr had missed her presentation, but he'd arrived in time for the awards dinner. People were mingling, their hands and claws full of appetizers and cocktails, or in a few cases, mugs of blood. The stone in his ring vibrated in warning at the close proximity of the demons, but thankfully it wasn't glowing. He'd gotten one of Azagoth's sons, Hawkyn, a Memitim skilled in alchemy, to temporarily change the properties of the surface of the diamond in order to conceal the color and the glow. He didn't want to take any chances that Jedda would recognize that the gemstone in his ring had been cut from the one she'd left with the Wardens.

The vibration grew stronger, becoming more of a pulse than a constant buzz. Odd. It only did that in the presence of its mate. Did it somehow recognize Jedda as the current owner of the larger stone? Had she...bonded with it?

Damn, he hoped not. If she had, the stone would need to be purified in the blood of a dying angel, which meant waiting like some kind of Heavenly vulture for a fellow angel to die.

Shit.

He swiped a glass of sparkling wine off a passing server's tray and cursed this stupid event. He hated parties. He especially hated demon parties. And this one was crawling with the suckers.

*Suck it up, cupcake. You are, perhaps, only mere minutes away from being reinstated as a full-fledged battle angel.*

Fresh enthusiasm sent a shiver of anticipation through him, even as his ring pulsed more feverishly. He looked around, seeking the source, and there, in the corner near the punch bowl, was Jedda.

And damn...she was...extraordinary. His breath clogged his throat as he took her in, because although he had known the greatest beauties to ever have existed both in the Heavenly realm and the human one, she was unique.

At least a foot shorter than he was and dressed in a stunning sapphire sheath that blurred the line between business-chic and cocktail dress, she was peering into her own glass of pink bubbly, her long, silver-blue hair framing a delicate face. As in the picture he'd seen of her in his mind and in her shop he'd visited before coming here, creamy skin glittered almost imperceptibly, and when she looked up, eyes that matched her hair glowed like twin gems.

Amazing.

She was a demon for sure, but what kind? He'd never seen anything like her.

He'd just started toward her when a hand came down on his shoulder from behind. Instinct kicked in, and he spun around, prepared to defend himself from whatever malevolent scumbag was trying to accost him. Instead, he found himself staring into a familiar face. A familiar *dead* face.

"Lexi? Is that...you?"

The pretty lion shapeshifter grinned and did a little twirl in her strapless red evening gown. "It's me," she said in her sing-songy Irish lilt. "In the flesh. Again."

*Again* was right. "I thought you died." He looked her up and down as if to reassure himself that she wasn't a ghost. He hadn't known her well, had only met her because her shifter pride had helped him follow a dead-end lead about his Enoch gem a while back. "I was told you'd been killed in a dance club explosion or something."

"Yeah," she sighed. "Thirst blew up and sort of dismembered me. But it turns out I have nine lives. And not because I'm a cat." She shrugged, her long brunette curls bouncing around her bare shoulders. "Evil witch, ancient curse, you know the drill."

"Sure, sure," he said absently, his gaze locking on Jedda again. Excitement surged through him now that his prey was nearby. "Excuse me," he said. "I need to see someone before I go." He gave her a brief hug. "It was good seeing you. Glad you're alive."

"Me too." She clanked her glass against his. "Enjoy your evening."

He moved toward Jedda, his pulse inexplicably growing faster as he neared her. He'd been in the presence of blindingly gorgeous females with unimaginable power in his centuries of life, and none of them had affected him like this. No, this was different, a mix of attraction and anticipation he would almost compare to battle lust.

The thought made him slow his approach, his mind tripping over the implications of that. Was he hoping she was one of the demons responsible for the theft of his property and the deaths of his friends, in which case he'd kill her, or was he hoping she wasn't involved? And which was worse? Oh, he had no problems with killing demons—it was what he'd been bred for. But it seemed like such a shame to slaughter someone so unique. Or so attractive.

*Idiot. You never drooled over demons when you were a full-fledged angel.*

No, he hadn't. There had been a clear separation of class and species back then. But ever since he'd had his wings bound and his powers muted and had been tossed in Sheoul-gra to serve Azagoth, he'd relaxed his standards. Not intentionally, but he had to admit that living life on the other side of the tracks had given him new perspective.

He just wasn't sure if that was a good thing or a bad one.

Jedda looked up as he stopped in front of her. Up close, she was even more beautiful, with full, pouty lips made to stir up some wicked male fantasies. Her fine, perfect features made her seem delicate, fragile, even, but something told him she was stronger than she looked. Which made him wonder how that strength would play in bed.

*Down, boy. Get what you want and get back to Heaven and females suited to your status.* And species. "Hello, Ms. Brighton. I'm Razr."

Cocking her head slightly, she gave him a long, assessing once-over before saying with just a hint of an English accent, "Razr? That's not a common human name, is it?"

Either she couldn't sense his species or she was testing him. Either way, he didn't see any reason to lie. "It's my fallen angel name. A take on my given name. Razriel."

"Ah." She gave him another long, measuring look, taking in the expensive suit Azagoth had given him for the event, and he wondered what she was thinking. "Until tonight, I'd never met a fallen angel, and now I've met two, including you."

"Tonight? Is the other one here?"

She nodded. "Shrike, the event organizer. He owns this place."

Well, that was mildly alarming. Fallen angels reveled in power and status, which meant that this shindig had probably been arranged for a purpose. An evil purpose.

"Huh," he said casually. "Never met him."

"I hadn't either until I agreed to speak at the conference. He seems...very intense." She paused to wave at someone near the grand piano. "Are all fallen angels like that?"

"There's a saying in Heaven," he said lightly. "Angels keep their humor in their wings."

"So when they get cut off..."

"So does their humor." He shrugged. "Of course, fallen angels do grow wings eventually."

"But their sense of humor doesn't grow back?"

"Oh, it does," he said, thinking of Azagoth and his pitch-black sense of humor. "You just don't want to be on the funny side of it."

She reached up and toyed with the multicolored choker around her slender neck, the dozens of rings on her fingers glinting in the light from the chandelier overhead. There were even little gemstones decorating her nails. She must be wearing a freaking fortune in jewels.

"Well, what about you?" she asked. "You seem to be a little less on the intense side."

He narrowed his eyes in mock suspicion, figuring that flirting might help get him what he wanted. Plus, as he'd already established, she was hot—for a demon. Especially for a demon. "Is 'intense' code for 'asshole'?"

She laughed, a delicate sound that was almost...musical. What kind of demon was she? A succubus, maybe? That would explain why he was picturing her tangled in bedsheets and why his cock was throbbing against the fabric of his pants.

"I say we change the subject." Still smiling, she took a sip of her drink. "So what brings you to the conference? Did you catch any of the panels?"

Panels? He could only imagine the topics at a place like this. *Plague Spells 101: The Pros and Cons of Magically-Enhanced Viruses. Warlocks and Witches and Sorcerers, Oh, My! Human Sacrifice: Yea or Nay?*

"No," he said, clearing his throat. "I just arrived, actually. I came to see you. Glad I tracked you down." Instantly, she lost the impish smile, and he cursed his mistake at making himself sound like an obsessed nut job.

"Tracked me down?" Even the temperature of her voice dropped a couple of frosty degrees.

"Not like a stalker or anything," he said hastily and in a bid to come off as charming. Not creepy.

He hoped.

"I went by your shop, but your staff told me you were giving a presentation tonight at a conference in Austria. Took it from there with research, and here I am." He put on his best chagrined face. "Not creepy at all."

She must have agreed, because there was a slight thaw in her eyes. "This is a very...exclusive...gathering, Mr. Razr. How did you arrange an invitation? Especially at the last minute?"

"I'm a fallen angel," he explained with a hint of fallen angel-like imperiousness. "I get what I want." Hadn't hurt that Azagoth let Razr do a little name-dropping, either. No one wanted to piss off the being who would eventually be in charge of their soul.

"Really." Her voice, now completely ice-free, went low, a caress that stroked him just under the skin. "Intriguing." She gave him a coy look as she lifted her glass to her mouth. "So why did you go to so much trouble to track me down?"

"I'm looking for a very special gemstone, and I hear you're the best at locating rare and precious stones."

"I am," she said with an arrogance he had to admire. "But why is this such an emergency that it couldn't wait until office hours tomorrow?"

"No emergency." He shifted closer to her, testing his boundaries. "It's just that I saw your picture at your shop and decided I didn't want to wait to meet you."

Her ruby lips curved in amusement. "Flattering. But you're avoiding the real question."

Lowering his voice to a conspiratorial whisper, he dipped his head closer to hers. "The room has ears." Most likely, anyway. Plus, he wanted to get her alone in case things got...complicated. She didn't reply, instead sipping at her drink as she eyed their surroundings. "I'm sorry... Did I say something wrong?"

"No." She stroked the stem of her glass, her jewel-encrusted fingernails reflecting the hall's flickering light in sparkly little bursts. "I'm just trying to decide if I should tell you to make an appointment or if I should suggest we go somewhere more private to talk."

Those nails. He was mesmerized, and his mind kept thinking about what they'd look like—and feel like—in places much more intimate than the stem of a champagne flute. Was she doing that on purpose? His dick sure thought so, and it tapped against the fly of his pants, begging for the same attention.

It was a damned good thing he'd buttoned his jacket.

"I vote for private," he said, his voice humiliatingly hoarse. He'd come over to seduce her, but she was clearly the one who held the cards in this game.

Succubus, for sure.

She made him sweat for a few seconds before finally nodding toward one of the exits. "I saw a balcony out that way." She started toward it, but a flash of light drew his attention, and he reached out to grab her elbow. "Wait."

"What is it?"

His gut churned as he checked out the next flash of light. Then the next and the next. Shit. Not good. He pulled her close and whispered into her ear. "Let's get out of here. Away from this conference."

"Aren't you naughty?"

"Yeah. Naughty. Let's go."

"But dinner is—"

He took her glass from her and placed both his and hers on a tray, his alarm growing as robed Ramreel demons with halberds began to station themselves around the room, the clop of their hooves ringing out over the sound of the guests and the music.

"Forget dinner."

"Look, I was invited for a reason," she snapped, clearly annoyed by his manhandling. "It would be rude to leave now."

He nonchalantly shifted his gaze to the four corners of the room, starting at the northern side. "See the glowing symbols painted on the walls?" At her nod, he continued. "Those symbolize sacrifice. Sacrifice to Lothar."

She frowned. "Who is Lothar?"

"How can you not know who Lothar is?" he asked, incredulous. Lothar was listed as one of the most famous scumbags in the first chapter of Demons For Dummies. "Didn't your demon parents teach you about the hundreds of patron fiends you can worship? You aren't limited to Satan, you know."

Her haughty sniff announced her irritation. "My parents didn't fill our heads with ridiculous fables—"

"They're not all fables. Definitely not this one." He tightened his grip on her arm and made a beeline for the exit. "Lothar is known as the Prince of Riches. A sacrifice to him gets you everything you want, and since you are one of the guests of honor..." He trailed off, letting her finish the thought. At her sharp inhale, he knew she'd pieced it together.

"I'm either part of the plan to get the riches...or I'm a sacrifice."

"Exactly."

"Well then," she said crisply, "I don't see why I need to hang around." Clever, how she made it sound like leaving had been her idea.

"That's what I've been trying to tell you," he ground out.

They'd nearly made it to the main doorway when a big blond male blocked their escape route. The dark energy emanating from him marked him as a fallen angel, which meant this could only be Shrike, the fallen angel who'd put this whole thing together.

"Leaving so soon?" His smile, showing way too many teeth and far too much of his gums, was as greasy as his slicked-back hair.

Razr was about to tell the guy to fuck off when Jedda offered an apologetic smile. "I have a family matter to attend to, Mr. Shrike," she said, inching closer to Razr. "And Razr kindly offered to escort me home."

Razr had to give her points for diplomacy, but Shrike didn't bite. "Unfortunately, I can't let you do that," he said. "The festivities are about to start, and I haven't had a chance to speak to you about my proposal."

"Yes, well, this is a bit of an emergency." Jedda adjusted her sparkly shoulder bag with an impatient tug. "Why don't we set up an appointment at my office for sometime this week?"

The smile on Shrike's face turned predatory, and Razr cursed inwardly. This was about to go south, and the bitch of it was that with Razr's angelic abilities bound, Shrike was a fuckton more powerful than Razr. Any negotiations would be all about Razr's ability to bluff his way through shit.

"As I said," Shrike practically purred, "the festivities are about to begin."

Suddenly, the lights shut off, leaving the space lit only by the flickering flames from the candles and torch sconces on the walls.

Yeah. *Real* south.

Speculative murmurs rose up, and unholy excitement charged the air.

"I don't like this," Jedda whispered, and Razr experienced the oddest desire to comfort her. To protect her. And not just because she was in possession of his gem. Heck, she might be responsible for stealing it and killing the humans who had been protecting it.

If so, he'd deal with it. But right now his only goal was to keep her safe.

And to get out of this alive.

# Chapter Five

Jedda had been in a lot of uncomfortable and downright dangerous situations before, but something about this one made the others, even the battles, seem tame.

Shrike wasn't your average Big Evil. He was Bigger Evil with an attitude. She had no idea what fallen angels were capable of, but it was probably safe to assume that they could make most demons look like kittens.

Razr, on the other hand... She wasn't sure what to think about him. He was smoking hot, for sure. She'd always been a sucker for dark hair and dark eyes, and she'd bet her life-stone that beneath his exquisitely tailored suit was the body of an athlete. He probably had amazing wings, too.

But there was also a familiarity between them that didn't make sense. She would have remembered meeting him, and yet she swore she felt a connection, as if their pulses were synced. And if that was true, then his pulse was pounding as hard as hers as she watched a bunch of blunt-snouted, horned dudes with wicked blades on the ends of long poles advance toward the center of the room. She thought the weapons were called halberds, but she supposed their name wasn't important. The fact that they could cleave a body in half was.

Razr moved close, and while Jedda was capable of taking care of herself in most circumstances, she had to admit to being grateful that he was, at least for now, her ally.

"Shrike," Razr growled. "What's going on—"

He broke off as, in a single, coordinated move, the halberd guys swung their blades so suddenly and so fast that she didn't have time to scream before a dozen heads plunked to the floor. Their owners' decapitated bodies collapsed next to them with wet, obscene thuds.

"Lexi!" A roar of rage tore from Razr's throat as a female in a crimson evening gown hit the tile, blood spurting from her headless neck.

Nausea and horror rolled through Jedda, and she stumbled backward as the shock wore off the crowd. Some people screamed, some cried, but most laughed.

Razr launched in a blur of fury. His fist slammed into Shrike's jaw, knocking him into a wall. Before Shrike could recover, Razr had Shrike by the throat and pinned, their faces nose to nose. "You killed her! What the fuck?"

"This *is* a demon dinner party," Shrike growled through bloodied lips. "What did you expect?" He smiled, one Jedda assumed was intended to be comforting but only came off as terrifying. "Besides, wasn't Lexi cursed with a bunch of lives and deaths? She'll pop up again somewhere." His eyes lit up with a malevolent crimson light, and little bursts of lightning sizzled at the tips of his fingers as he raised his hand toward the back of Razr's head. "But you won't."

"No!" Jedda shouted. "Don't do it, Shrike. He's with me, and if you kill him, I swear that whatever 'proposal' you have for me is going to die with him. I will *never* work with you."

Shrike snorted, but he dropped his hand to his side again. "I think you will. But I'll let him live. For now."

The crowd began to chant a bunch of mumbo-jumbo Jedda didn't recognize, but she did understand one word: Lothar. Her gut churned again.

"Fuck you." Razr shoved Shrike hard enough to make his skull crack against the wall. "Let us leave, you piece of shit. The ceremony is over."

One of Shrike's hooded goons spotted his boss's predicament and headed their way, the edge of his blade dripping with blood. Jedda forced her wobbly legs to move closer to Razr so she could tap him on the shoulder and impress upon him the urgency of their situation. Shrike might have shelved his homicidal urges for the moment, but he seemed like the kind of psycho who could change his mind in an instant. "Hey, maybe you should back off a little..."

"You really have no choice but to release me." Shrike's deceptively calm voice wigged Jedda out. In her experience, hotheads were far better to deal with than people whose emotions ran cold. Both could be dangerous, but hotheads were more predictable and easier to manipulate. Shrike didn't strike her as either of those things. He gestured toward a closed door nearby. "Why don't we go someplace quieter to talk?"

Razr hesitated. He was going to refuse and get them both killed, wasn't he? Man, she'd been sealed inside collapsed diamond mines and had never felt this trapped. Finally, just as she was counting the number of goons between her and the nearest door, Razr cursed and backed off. What he didn't do was stop glaring daggers at the other fallen angel. Not even while Shrike led them to a grand library full of literary classics, modern fiction, and a sprinkling of demonic tomes.

Seething at Shrike's trickery and betrayal, and still hopped up on an adrenaline dump, she rounded on the bastard as soon as the door closed. "What is it you want, Mr. Shrike? And why didn't you simply make an appointment instead of inviting me here for this...this...spectacle?"

She looked over at Razr, who stood a couple of feet away, his fists clenched at his sides and his dark eyes smoldering. Hatred practically seeped from his pores, and she swore she could feel it in a wave of acid heat washing over her skin.

Shrike walked around the desk and sank into the leather chair behind it. He gestured for both her and Razr to take seats in the two chairs across from him. She accepted, but Razr shot the other fallen angel the bird and remained standing, his gaze sharp, his stance deceptively relaxed. Jedda got the impression that inside he was coiled like a snake and ready to strike.

Shrike shot Razr an annoyed glance but then focused on Jedda. "I invited you here because the things I'm going to ask you for aren't going to be easy to find. Hence, the sacrifice. It's important that its energy envelops you."

*Evil bastard.* Jedda didn't have a whole lot of room to lecture anyone on the subject of ethics, but she'd never tricked anyone into attending a murder-themed dinner party.

*No, but you've killed too.*

Dammit, no she hadn't. Not intentionally.

But she'd benefited from the death, hadn't she?

Shoving her errant thoughts back into the deepest recesses of her mind where they belonged, she looked Shrike in his steel-gray eyes. "I don't appreciate the deception," she said in her brisk business voice, the one she used when dealing with deplorable people like Tom from the Taaffeite mine. "And I definitely don't appreciate being enveloped in some strange spell. So I don't think I'll be doing business with you." She started to stand, but lightning fast, his big hand clamped around her wrist.

A snarl rang out, freezing her in her seat more effectively than Shrike's grip ever could.

*"Release her."* Razr's eyes glittered with the threat of violence. It made her wonder what fallen angels were capable of. And it was a little bit of a turn-on.

Shrike grinned, a smile so cold she shivered. "As long as she promises to hear me out."

Shit. She didn't want to hear another word from this bin of burning rubbish, but she also didn't have a death wish, nor did she want to see Razr flopping around on the floor next to his head.

"Of course," she agreed with forced calm, hoping to alleviate the tension and get this meeting over with. "I suppose it can't hurt."

"Good." Shrike released her, and she resisted the urge to rub her wrist, where her skin burned as if his fingers had been sticks of fire. "Now, here's the deal. What I want will be a challenge, but I know you'll come through for me."

"Just tell me what it is, and I'll tell you if I think it's possible."

For some reason, he looked amused, and she didn't like that one bit. "You are, of course, familiar with the famous crystal skulls of Mesoamerica."

She couldn't stop herself from rolling her eyes. Not only was every one of them almost certainly fake, but if he wanted one he could easily hire any competent dealer in antiquities. He didn't need her for that. "Of course. But—"

"Are you also familiar with the crystal devil's horns?"

She sucked in a startled breath. The existence of the crystal devil's horns wasn't common knowledge. Even most of those who were familiar with the legends didn't believe they existed.

"I'm sorry," Razr said, "but what the fuck is a crystal devil's horn?"

Shrike sat back, the smug look on his face so obnoxious she wanted to slap it off. "Not long after the first crystal skulls came onto the scene, a human archaeologist digging in Mexico discovered a curved crystal horn, much like a ram's horn. It was perfectly seamless, with no flaws."

Jedda leaned forward eagerly, unable to contain her excitement. She loved mysteries that surrounded the elements of the earth. "It was found deep inside a cave full of human skeletons, and it was reportedly hot to the touch. The man who found it went insane shortly afterward, and the horn was lost to the ages. But then, in 1938, Adolf Hitler sent a team to the same cave in search of more treasures. They found another horn, and they assumed that it, along with the first one, belonged to a crystal skull. But no skull that matched the horns was ever found."

Shrike shook his head. "A skull was found." He dug into his desk drawer and pulled out a black and white photo of what she could only describe as a crystal skull. A crystal *demon* skull.

"That's incredible," she murmured. "All the other skulls are human, or at least primate in nature. But this looks like something you'd find in a demon graveyard." Its long, pointed chin and sharp teeth gave it a monstrous profile, and two perfectly round indentions at the temples appeared to be the perfect resting places for horns.

Razr strode over and pulled the photo to the edge of the desk. "Where is it now?"

"According to my sources, Satan himself owns it." At Razr's snort, Shrike took insult, his mouth tightening in a grim line. "You have something to add?"

"No," Razr said, the odd note in his voice making Jedda suspect he knew something pertinent to this conversation. "It's just that Satan hasn't been seen in a while."

Shrike tapped his long fingers on the desktop. "So you believe the rumors that he's been usurped?"

Usurped? Jedda hadn't heard that. But then, she'd never, not in her hundred and forty years of life, been interested in the politics of the Heavenly, human, or demonic realms unless they affected her directly. Heck, she was barely interested in her own species' politics.

At Razr's casual shrug, she sighed. "Look, I don't know what you want me to do about this. You'd be better off hiring someone who locates antiquities. I'm a gemologist. I specialize in finding gems that are still rough in the earth or that have been enhanced with supernatural abilities."

"Don't toy with me, sweetheart. I know you deal in all gems. And the devil's horn is one of the most precious."

Shit. How could she get out of this without revealing the truth— that certain types of crystal were beyond her ability to sense? Not only that, but quartz crystal, like that associated with the skulls and the horns, might as well be her kryptonite? She'd learned that in the most embarrassing way imaginable.

"Mr. Shrike, only two horns are believed to exist. I'm not sure I can find either one of them." She cleared her throat. "And I'm certain that I won't find them if you call me sweetheart again."

He laughed, but she'd expected no less. "I have faith in you. But I'm not finished." He braced his forearms on the desk and leaned forward. "There's something else I want."

Of course there was.

"Have you heard of the Gems of Enoch?"

Her heart stopped. Just...stopped. Her chest tightened, her breath burned, and her stomach dropped to her feet. Beneath her skin, she felt her panic response rise up, and she had to force herself to calm the hell down.

And was it her imagination or did she see Razr tense up out of the corner of her eye? Had to be her imagination. Unless he sensed the sudden, cold terror inside her?

She hid her anxiety behind a forced laugh. "Mr. Shrike. Surely you don't believe that silly legend."

"It's no legend." Shrike's brows slammed down in annoyance. "Three gemstones made of angel blood and tears. Each was rumored to possess different powers, and each was placed in an angel's care. These gemstones, when activated together, formed powerful magic. But around a century ago, three extraordinarily powerful demons defeated the angels and stole the gems."

He was right about the stones, but he'd gotten the story wrong. Very wrong. "I'm sorry," she said, "but I'm not wasting my time on a silly goose chase."

"It's true," Razr chimed in, not helping her at all. "At least, the existence of the stones is reality." He wandered around the library, his gaze seeming to take in everything at once, and Jedda got the feeling he was committing every tome and every artifact on display to memory. "Shrike fucked up the story though."

"Really." Shrike glared. "Maybe you could tell me where I went wrong and how you know this?"

"The exploits of the angels who used the gems in battle are well-recorded in Heaven's Akashic Library, and I like to read." Razr ran his hand over a pile of books on the table near the window. "According to several accounts, demons didn't defeat the angels. Demons murdered the humans who were the custodians of the gems."

Well, that was a little closer to the truth, she supposed. But only one human had been killed, and the guilt weighed on her like a two-ton boulder.

Shrike gave a skeptical snort. "Why would angels need human custodians?"

"Because the power contained in the stones needs a conduit." Jedda immediately cursed her loose lips. "At least, that's according to the legends," she added quickly.

Storm clouds gathered in Shrike's eyes and his fingernails dug into the desktop. "It appears that my source hasn't been entirely forthcoming with information," he ground out, and man, she wouldn't want to be that source. Then, just as quickly as the storm came in, it passed, and Shrike looked between Razr and Jedda. "If humans hold the gemstones, how do the angels draw on the power?"

"I don't know," Razr replied as he flipped through a book about carnivorous vegetation in the demon realm. "I didn't get that far in my reading."

Jedda knew the answer to Shrike's question, but she didn't feel like sharing. Hell, she didn't feel like *remembering* that the angels wore special jewelry made from their corresponding gemstone. The angel who had murdered Jedda's sister had worn an amethyst charm around his neck that matched the stone Manda possessed.

*"This,"* Ebel said as he rubbed his finger across his necklace's pendant, *"allows me to tap into the power of the gem I know is in your possession."*

*He looked at Jedda, Manda, and Reina in turn, his icy gaze sending a tingle of dread skittering up Jedda's spine. He'd caught them in the house they'd shared, a sprawling seventeenth century French manor that had belonged to their deceased parents.*

*"Where is it? Where are all three of them?" He moved toward Manda as she cowered in the corner, his booted foot coming down in the puddles of blood and gems spilled all over the floor. "I sense mine. You reek of it. I want it back."*

*"She can't give it to you!" Reina screamed. "It's impossible."*

*He grinned, and around his neck, the amethyst charm glowed. Suddenly, his hand flew out, and a gash, larger than the others he'd inflicted, split Manda's skin from her shoulder to her elbow. She shrieked in pain as blood streamed down her arm and pooled on the floor. Gems formed in the blood, some no larger than a karat in size, while others, like the duck-egg sized enchanted lapis they'd stolen from a vampire a couple of decades before were more impressive.*

*Which was bad. The larger the stones that formed outside her body, the more damage was being done to the inside of her body.*

*"Do you want to understand the full power of the gems?" he asked silkily, and no, Jedda really did not. She and her sisters had each claimed a stone and absorbed its considerable energy. That energy had given them abilities they hadn't possessed before, but they'd been aware that the power of the gems wouldn't be fully unlocked without their mates, and now it looked like they were going to find out how powerful those things were.*

Screams blasted through Jedda's brain, screams that belonged to her sisters, herself...no, wait...

She blinked, realizing she'd been lost in the past, when right here in the present people were screaming from beyond the door. Shrike was grinning.

"More sacrifices," he purred, the ecstasy in his voice almost as disturbing as what was happening in the other room. "Lothar is demanding. And with every scream, his will is seeping into you."

Horror left her struggling to breathe. "What...what do you mean?"

"I mean that every day that passes without you bringing me what

I desire will cause more and more misery for you. Don't worry, it won't kill you. But before the month is out, you'll wish it would."

Razr tossed the book onto the pile on the table and spun around. "You sick fuck." He twisted the ring on his finger as if trying to find something to do with his hands that wouldn't involve strangling the bastard sitting across from them.

Jedda voted for the strangling.

Shrike's eyebrows climbed up his forehead. "You're a fallen fucking angel." He sneered. "An Unfallen, I suspect, but you still fucked up enough to get kicked out of Heaven. So don't tell me you've never killed anyone."

Razr's voice went low and ominous, and the hair on Jedda's neck stood up. "As an angel I killed thousands of fiends like you. Some of them even deserved it."

"So will Jedda," Shrike said, "if she doesn't bring me what I want." He speared her with a look that promised agony on a grand scale. "And you will update me daily on your progress, or I'll send my men to deal with you."

*Son of a bitch.* This was why she was in business for herself. Why she refused to work for anyone except on her own terms. She didn't like being controlled or tied to anyone, and what Shrike was doing both tied her to him and controlled her choices for the next month, at the very least.

Fury scorched her throat with every word. "So you brought me here under false pretenses in order to force me to do your bidding?"

"This wasn't entirely a ruse." Shrike steepled his hands on his desk, his countenance so laid back that she got the impression he fucked people over a lot. And got off on it. "I do sponsor a legitimate annual sorcery conference. You can Google it."

She had, which was why she'd felt comfortable attending. "I'm so going to destroy you on Yelp," she snapped.

Razr laughed, but it abruptly cut off as he glanced down at the back of his hand, where the raised outline of what looked like a wing was glowing with an eerie crimson light. Had it been there earlier? She didn't think so.

"Well, well," Shrike murmured. "An *Azdai* glyph."

Razr's gaze snapped up to meet Shrike's. "What do you know about *Azdai* glyphs?"

"I know more than I should." Shrike's expression softened, even as his voice grew bitter, leaving Jedda more confused than ever.

"I need to go." Razr made a "come with" gesture to Jedda and started toward the exit, but Shrike shook his head and the clank of a heavy lock sliding into place rattled the door.

"We aren't finished here."

Razr wheeled around with a hiss. "If you know anything about *Azdai* glyphs, you know I have to."

"I know you need someone to deliver your punishment." Shrike came smoothly to his feet. "I'll do the honors." He held out his hand. "I owe you for the right hook and the cracked skull."

"Go to hell."

"Once again, I'll point out that you have no choice. This castle is on lockdown and I just decided to keep it that way until you agree."

"What is going on?" Jedda demanded. "I don't understand any of this."

Razr explained, but his gaze remained locked with Shrike's, a battle of wills that she had a feeling wasn't going to end well.

"Azdai was an angel before humans even knew what angels were. Before the rebellion that got Satan thrown out of Heaven." Razr sucked air between his teeth as if he was in pain, but Jedda had no idea what could be hurting him. "Azdai hurt humans in the way human children sometimes pull the wings off flies. He was curious and cruel, and he had to be punished. Fallen angels didn't exist yet, so Heaven came up with this glyph and the punishment that goes with it." He held up his hand, where the feather-shaped glyph burned bright crimson, so angry she flinched. "When it lights up, it means that it's time to experience punishment. If the punishment doesn't take place immediately, we suffer until some asshole angel shows up to inflict the punishment tenfold." He reached into his jacket pocket and pulled out the most beautiful ivory-handled cat-o'-nine tails she'd ever seen. Even the little bone spurs on the ends of the leather strands had been polished to gleaming perfection. "And we can't inflict the punishment ourselves." He unfolded the compact handle and locked it into place, and then he passed the torture device to Shrike. Jedda's stomach turned over at the realization that the cat was about to be used. "We earn extra credit when the punisher is merciless."

"Extra credit?" she asked, feeling utterly sick.

"We can go longer between beatings."

She put her hand over her belly, but it didn't quell the nausea. "That's...barbaric."

"You'll get no argument from me," Razr said as he removed his jacket and shirt. As she suspected, he was as fit as an athlete, his well-muscled broad chest tapering to a narrow waist and abs she'd bet would make diamonds seem soft in comparison.

"Wait." She leaped to her feet and tried to reason with Shrike. "Don't do this," she pleaded. "I'll do whatever you want. I'll do my best to find the items you want—"

"You're already going to do that," Shrike said.

She looked over at Razr, who was now removing the various weapons strapped around his hips and looking at her like she was crazy for wanting to help him. She kind of felt that way, she supposed. This was none of her business. Heck, she didn't know why he was even in the office in the first place except that, oh, right, he'd tried to save her from the Dinner Party From Hell and had gotten caught up in the trap Shrike had set for her. So, yeah, this was all her fault, and she didn't want to see Razr hurt.

"What can I do?"

Razr flung his clothes and half a dozen blades onto a chair. "You can make sure this asshole doesn't fuck with me when I pass out."

With that, he reached out and grabbed the wall.

# Chapter Six

This sucked. Usually Razr's punishment came from Azagoth or Hades, although Zhubaal had filled in a couple of times. Z didn't like it, not like Azagoth and Hades, who both seemed to enjoy doling out a little torture, even among friends, but sometimes things couldn't be helped.

"Please," Jedda whispered as Shrike's heavy steps crossed the room. "Surely this can wait—"

"It can't," Shrike said, his eyes glowing with that unholy crimson light again. "Even now, he's feeling pressure build inside. His skin is burning. His blood feels like lava. Every minute without punishment increases the agony. Isn't that right, Razr?"

Unfortunately, yes. "How the fuck do you know?"

Shrike stroked his finger over the cat-o'-nine's smooth handle, and how fucked up was it that Razr actually experienced jealousy? He hated the cat. But it was *his*, and he despised the fact that this fallen angel fuckwad was caressing it.

Yeah, fucked up.

Shrike's voice was soft, almost...tender. "Does it matter how I know?"

Not really, but Razr guessed there was one hell of a story behind his knowledge. "Just get it over with. Six of them."

"No!" Jedda put herself between Razr and Shrike. What the hell was she doing? He was a stranger to her, and yet she was trying to protect him.

Unaccustomed to being the recipient of such kindness, he hung his head, at a loss for how to handle this. His wings, bound so tightly that they ached, quivered under his skin as if wanting to erupt from his back and shield her from what she was about to witness.

He lifted his head and looked at her from over his shoulder. "Jedda," he said roughly, "it's okay. Don't look. It'll be over quickly."

For the span of a dozen heartbeats she hesitated. And then, reluctantly, she nodded and moved aside for Shrike, but she still cried out as the first blow fell across his shoulders, which, although fully healed, were still sensitive from the last flogging he'd taken at Jim Bob's hand.

Pain exploded and blood splattered. He clenched his teeth and bore the second blow with a grunt. His ears rang, but through the buzz he could hear Jedda pleading with Shrike to stop.

Nothing she said would stop him. She *couldn't* stop him. This was something Razr had earned, and he'd learned the hard way that it was much less painful to take the blows than to suffer for days sometimes until an angel showed up to flay him with ten times the number of strikes.

Sixty fucking blows.

He normally healed within a few hours, but it took him days to recover from that kind of angel-inflicted torture.

Another blow landed, and his vision blurred.

He didn't even feel the next one.

\* \* \* \*

"Gods, you're heavy. You're damned lucky my species is freakishly strong." He was also lucky that there was a Harrowgate just a block away from Jedda's house or she'd have been forced to explain to a taxi driver why she was hauling around an unconscious, bloody man in the middle of the night.

She gasped with effort as she unceremoniously dumped Razr's unconscious body onto her bed, and so much for her new jade and amethyst comforter and sheets. All ruined by sticky smears of blood.

What was up with that, anyway? Why had Razr needed to be tortured? And why did she care? She hadn't cared about anyone since the day an angel killed one sister and sent the other into the wind. She'd been lonely at times, but mostly being alone meant not having to compete with anyone else for anything. Like the gems that kept her alive.

Oh, their parents had planned ahead of time to avoid competition between Jedda and her sisters, and for the most part it had worked. But her species was naturally competitive, and honestly, she was surprised that she and her siblings had stuck together for as long as they had. Most gem elf siblings lost touch within a couple of years of reaching adulthood at the age of sixteen human years.

She wondered where Reina was, if she was even still in the human realm. The last time Jedda had seen her sister had been a decade ago at an underworld gem and weapons show on the outskirts of the Ca'askull region of Sheoul. They'd run into each other at a display booth for cursed magnetite, and it had done nothing to heal the hurt between them.

Absolutely nothing. Reina knew how to contact Jedda, but she hadn't.

Not that Jedda was totally blameless. She'd followed up once, but after finding that Reina no longer lived at the location she'd given Jedda, she'd given up. Sure, she could attend the weekly gem trade in the elven realm where Reina would surely be on a regular basis, but Jedda was stubborn, and she wasn't going to be the one to make overtures at this point.

A sound outside her front door followed by a wave of intense evil jolted her out of her thoughts and raised the hackles on the back of her neck. Silently, she slipped to the living room window and peeked between the sapphire curtains. There, hanging in the shadows just off her porch, was a demon she recognized from the sacrificial dinner. He just stood there, his back against the side of the house as he looked out toward the street.

What the hell?

She whipped open the door. "What are you doing?"

He turned to her, flashing sharp, ugly teeth. "Shrike wants me to keep an eye on you. Make sure you deliver what you promised."

"Tell Shrike he can go fuck himself. I don't need a babysitter."

The bastard started toward her, but screw that. She wasn't giving him a chance to so much as lay a finger on her. Throwing out her hand, she summoned the power of the very gem Shrike wanted her to find, the ice-blue diamond of myth and legend. All around her the air shimmered as heat built. With a mere thought, she released the energy, hitting him with a shockwave that sent him tumbling all the way to the street, where he landed in an awkward heap against a lamp pole.

"Stay off my property," she shouted. "Or next time that wave will take you apart." It wasn't true, but he didn't need to know that. Oh, she could have summoned twice as much power, but she lived in a human neighborhood, and there was no sense in drawing attention to herself. Especially since many humans were aware of the existence of the supernatural thanks to recent near-apocalyptic events, and nothing good ever came of humans and their fear.

Still, she'd always wondered how truly powerful her gem would be if paired with its mate and the angel who possessed it. Before he killed Manda, Ebel the Angry Angel had said that the paired gems were capable of widespread destruction on an atomic level, and she believed it. Even now she could feel her gem's power like a pulse inside her, as if it wanted to unleash everything it was capable of.

Shivering, she went back inside and fetched the med kit from the bathroom. Razr was still passed out cold, so she gently stripped off his slacks.

He didn't wear underwear. *Oh, my.*

Her mouth went as dry as the sand forest in her elven homeland as she took in his magnificent body. Everything began to burn, parts of her she'd all but forgotten she had in the five years since she'd last been with a man. The fallen angel was about as perfect as anything she'd ever seen. Made sense, she supposed—she'd never thought angels would be anything less than perfection. But seeing one naked and up close? No one could blame her for wanting to take pictures and post to all her friends on Instagram, right?

Cursing her ethics, she arranged him on his belly to allow access to his shredded back. Shame at the fact that she'd just ogled him shrank her skin. Gods, he must have been in so much pain. She'd nearly passed out herself during the beating, unable to stomach the sight of muscle and bone exposed by the deep lacerations.

Making matters worse, Shrike had reveled in the gore, growing angrier with each strike, as if he'd been taking some deep inner pain out on Razr. When it was over, he'd thrown down the cat and fled the office without a word, leaving her to gather Razr's unconscious body and find her way out of the castle.

At least the wounds had stopped bleeding and were already starting to heal. Still, this was one of the times she wished she'd chosen the garnet Gem of Enoch instead of the diamond. Jedda and her sisters hadn't known what power each of the gems had possessed at the time they'd chosen and assimilated them, but neither Jedda nor Reina had been completely happy with the outcomes. Manda had embraced the killing power of her stone, but Reina had no desire to heal anyone and had been furious. And while Jedda's gem had given her an ability to violently repel demons that she actually used sometimes, being able to help now and then would have been cool too.

Very carefully, she cleaned Razr's wounds and applied bandages, each one drawing an elven curse from her. Such a perfect body, torn to shreds on a regular basis. He had no scars—at least, none that were visible. She'd heard there were species of demons that could see scars no one else could, and she wondered what one of those demons would see if they looked at Razr.

Jedda saw a very fit, very toned male.

Bronzed skin stretched over thick veins that helped define the sharp-cut muscles of his shoulders and arms, and if there was an ounce of fat on his body, she'd turn her jewelry store into a yogurt shop.

Tenderly, she ran her fingers over his biceps and forearm, all the way to his fingers. His ring fascinated her, and when she touched the black diamond in the center, she felt the oddest buzz, as if it contained an enchantment that was restrained and trying to get out. Even stranger, enchanted gemstones were always aligned with good, evil, or neutral energy, and she couldn't get any kind of read on it. Was he aware of its potential power? Or its alignment?

Putting her questions aside, she followed a thick vein up the back of his hand and then laid her hand over his, marveling at how much bigger his was. As an elf, she was naturally on the delicate side, but he truly created a stark contrast in not only their size, but their coloring. Where she was light, he was dark.

Even the tattoos that looped around his shoulder blades and ran up the back of his neck in twin Celtic-style braids before disappearing under short-cropped black hair were dark. Not in color—although they were deep blue—but in nature. She recognized the symbols woven into the rope-like pattern. They were often burned or carved into objects, like cursed or enchanted gemstones, to dampen their power.

Were Razr's tattoos more punishment for whatever he'd done?

Gods, what *had* he done? It had to have been bad to get kicked out of Heaven, but then to be saddled with extra punishment?

She eyed the door. Maybe she'd made a mistake bringing him home. She'd heard there was a clinic right here in London that treated demons and fallen angels and the like... She could drop him off and then check on him tomorrow.

He shifted, wincing at the slightest motion, and she sighed in resignation. After all, a girl had to bring home the wrong guy at least once in her life, didn't she? And hey, he'd tried to warn her, tried to get her out of the dinner party before everything went to hell. If she'd listened instead of arguing, maybe she wouldn't be in this mess.

She owed him for trying.

Plus, he seemed to know a lot about the Gems of Enoch. It made her a little nervous, but at the same time, she'd love to learn more. She and her sisters had only discovered them because they'd felt them in use, and they'd stolen them before they'd learned what they were. Since that day a century ago, Jedda had done as much research as possible, but very little was known about them.

Seemed that very few angels published books about their greatest weapons. Go figure.

After she finished patching him up, she went to the kitchen to prepare something to eat and to plan her next move. Clearly Shrike was serious about getting what he wanted, and if he'd really enveloped her in some sort of sacrificial demonic magic, she was in trouble. Maybe she could get her hands on the horn he wanted, but there was no way she could give him her gem, even if she wanted to. It was part of her. It was why her heart was beating and her blood was pumping.

Without it, she would die. The thing that sucked, though, was that if she didn't give it to him, the result would probably be the same.

# Chapter Seven

Coffee. Fuck, Razr needed coffee.

That was always his first thought when he woke up. Even as an angel waking up in Heaven, he'd wanted that uniquely human beverage that so many of his angelic brethren turned their noses up at. Hot, cold, black, with milk...it didn't matter to Razr. Just hand it over or get out of the way.

He yawned, opened his eyes and blinked, startled at the sight of Jedda sitting in a chair next to the bed he was currently sprawling in. He'd dreamed about her, except she hadn't been wearing a bright turquoise silk blouse and shimmering black leggings that showed off toned thighs and calves like she was now.

She'd been naked. Her luxurious silver-blue hair had blanketed her perky breasts, but everything else had been gloriously free of any kind of covering. She'd been walking on a beach of white sand and pink shells, and as she sauntered up to him, she'd held out his Enoch diamond.

Razr had extended his hand... But he still didn't know if he'd been wanting the gem—or her. The dream had flickered away as consciousness interrupted.

"Hey, you." Jedda reached for a pitcher of water on the bedside table. "You weren't out as long as I thought you'd be. You heal fast."

Confused, he rolled onto his side and pushed up on an elbow, feeling the pinch of something on his back. Bandages. She'd bandaged him? "Where am I?"

"I brought you to my place." She poured water into a glass and handed it to him. "I couldn't just leave you there bleeding on Shrike's floor. Who knows what he'd have done to you?"

His stomach rumbled—he'd missed the sacrificial dinner, after all—and he took a drink of water to quell it. It wasn't coffee, but he wasn't going to complain to someone who had helped him out.

"Where are my weapons and clothes?" When she pointed at a pile on the floor, he relaxed and set the glass down. "How did you get me here? And where *is* here?"

She offered a small smile. "I'm stronger than I look, and *here* is London."

Oh, right. He'd gotten that info when he'd gone to Scotland. "Near your shop?"

She shrugged. "It's walking distance in good weather. One stop on the Tube in bad weather. But this *is* England, so I ride the Tube a lot." She made a circular gesture with one bejeweled finger. Besides her gem-encrusted fingernails, she wore a lot of rings. As many as three on each finger. "Turn over and I'll remove the bandages."

He could do it himself, and he didn't generally like taking orders, but he suddenly wanted very much to have her tending to him. Touching him. The dream was still fresh in his mind, so what the hell.

Besides, while it was technically forbidden for angels to fraternize with demons, he was, for all intents and purposes, considered a fallen angel. Which meant all bets were off, and Heaven could suck it.

*She* could suck it.

Groaning at the inappropriately erotic thought, he flipped onto his stomach, and oh, look at that, he was naked. She'd stripped him bare and he hadn't awakened? That had happened only once before, when Zhubaal had carried him from Azagoth's office after a particularly brutal flogging and laid him out on his bed in Sheoul-gra. He'd awakened confused and sore, but at least he'd been in his own bed.

"So." The mattress dipped as she sat next to him, her warm thigh pressing against his hip through the purple satin sheet. She liked her jewel tones, didn't she? Everything in the room, from the bright citrine lampshade to the jade rug and ruby wall accents screamed, *I hate subtle color and earth tones.* "What's the deal with this punishment thing?"

His cheeks heated with humiliation. "I did something stupid, and I got in trouble for it."

"Yeah, I guessed that much. Must have been pretty bad to get you kicked out of Heaven and to be cursed with eternal punishment."

"I also spent a few decades in prison," he muttered into the pillow.

His two team members, Ebel and Darlah, had rotted in jail with him while all their fates were decided. Ebel had been released first, with no restrictions on his power and without an *Azdai* glyph. It had taken him only two years to track down his gemstone and destroy one of the thieves who'd stolen it from him, but the amethyst had been tainted by the evil of the one who had possessed it, an evil that darkened his soul and turned him against his own kind.

He'd been hunted down and slaughtered. His gem and his pendant now sat uselessly in some archangel's office until the other two Gems of Enoch could be recovered and a new team could be formed.

Next, they'd released Darlah to find her gem, but this time, she'd been hobbled like Razr, her wings—and consequently, her power—bound, and she'd been branded with an *Azdai* glyph.

She'd disappeared three years later and was presumed dead.

Now it was Razr's turn. Returning to Heaven with his gem would redeem him. Returning with both his diamond and Darlah's garnet would make him a hero. Heaven would once again have the three Enoch stones, and he could put together another team to combat demons.

He *needed* those stones, and one was within his grasp. He just had to exercise a little patience and be smart.

Jedda's finger smoothed over the bandages, and he nearly purred. No one had touched him like that since Darlah. And even then, their relationship had been sexual, frantic, and intense, with zero intimate moments. At least, not by his definition of intimate.

"Can I ask what you did?"

He inhaled sharply, wondering how to play this. He could lie, tell the truth, employ avoidance... He had a few options. In the end, he settled on a generic version of the truth, figuring that offering a little information might help him draw info out of her, as well.

"I was part of an elite demon-slaying team. We got careless one day, and our carelessness cost lives and property."

Anger and regret burned through his veins at the memory. They'd been battling hordes of demons advancing on a shithole village in what was now Somalia, and Razr had ordered Ebel to station the stones and their human guardians on the edge of town near Razr and his team. But Ebel had misunderstood, placing the trio of humans and gems in the center of town, leaving them out of sight and vulnerable to demons who somehow slipped through the barrier generated by Razr's Enoch diamond. It had been a clusterfuck of epic proportions, and one Razr would never forget. Not even his dreams gave him respite from the sight of the death and destruction.

"I'm sorry," Jedda said softly. "I know exactly what that's like. I lost my entire family because I was careless too."

"They're dead?"

She peeled a bandage away with surprising tenderness. He'd have ripped the sucker off. "My parents and one sister are. My other sister and I might as well be strangers."

Okay, so now he *had* to know. "What kind of demon are you?"

She shifted, planting one warm palm on his waist, and his body stirred to sudden, hot life. Beneath his hips, his shaft swelled, and the satiny sheet rubbing it like a caress made it even worse.

"I'm not a demon."

He laughed. "Bullshit."

"I'm not." She pulled off another strip of bandage, and he welcomed the slight burn of the adhesive tugging on his skin. He needed the distraction. Badly. "I'm a gem elf."

"A what?" Talk about a distraction.

"A gem elf," she said slowly, as if he was hard of hearing. Or a toddler.

"I heard you. I just don't know what a gem elf is."

"Aren't angels supposed to know everything?"

How cute. Angels seemed to be kept in the dark about everything. "Obviously not," he said, adjusting his hips to accommodate his pinched erection. "But I do know you're a demon."

She removed another bandage, this time less gently. A lot less gently. "I think I'd know if I was a demon."

"How would you know?" he shot back. "Does a giraffe know it's a giraffe? Have you been classified by science or Baradoc, the demonologist?"

She huffed in indignation, and he hid his smile in the pillow. "My people aren't part of the demon or human worlds. We don't have any kind of corresponding religions or lore. We even have our own realm."

He snorted. "Angels don't know everything, but we *are* familiar with all the realms. If there was an elven realm, I'd know."

"That's pretty arrogant."

He shrugged. "What can I say? I'm an angel. A fallen angel," he corrected.

"Angel or not, you're an asshole," she muttered, and he laughed. She was adorable. And clearly, a demon. So was she lying to him or did she truly believe she was an elf?

A fucking *elf*. Ridiculous.

Her fingers fluttered over his bare shoulder blades, and he went taut at the first probe of the scar-like streaks from which his wings would emerge if they weren't bound.

"What are these?"

"Those are wing anchors."

"That's where they cut your wings off?" There was a startling note of sadness in her voice that left him off balance. She didn't know him. Not really. And yet, she felt bad for him? "I'd have thought they'd have healed by now. When did you fall?"

"A couple of years ago," he hedged, not wanting to get into this, especially because his wings hadn't been severed. Just bound so tightly with special golden twine that they ached every minute of every day.

"But the stitches—"

He sat up quickly to change the subject, but the sudden move knocked her off balance and sent her sprawling on the floor. Right on top of the insanely bright rug.

"Oh, shit." He leaped off the bed to help her up. "Sorry. I..." He trailed off as he lifted her to her feet, the look on her face as she stared at him leaving him even more off balance than before.

Those amazing eyes glittered as she took in his nudity. His cock, already rock hard, jerked under her gaze. Desire hammered through him, becoming a rapid pounding in his groin that grew more intense the longer they stood there, both frozen by what was happening.

He wanted her. He'd wanted her since the first moment he'd seen her, even though he'd believed that things could only end badly between them. Especially if she was responsible for the theft of his gem and the death of its human host, a young man named Nabebe whom Razr had all but raised.

But dammit, he liked Jedda, and he was beginning to doubt she'd had anything to do with the events that got him banished from Heaven. As a gem dealer, she could have acquired the Enoch diamond at any time during the last century or so, and it made sense that she'd deny knowing anything about it, given that the most powerful forces in Heaven and Sheoul were after it. Hell, Razr had even heard that Satan had put out feelers before he was locked away by Revenant, Sheoul's new king, and his brother, Reaver, the most famous battle angel in history.

*But she's a demon. You hate demons. You were born to fight them. To destroy them.*

Yes, that was true. But during Razr's service to Azagoth, he'd been around enough demons to know that they weren't one-size-fits-all. Baby battle angels cut their teeth on the knowledge that all demons were pure evil and must be destroyed, but he knew better now. Just like humans, each demon was unique down to the depth of malice or decency in their souls.

He'd bet that Jedda was one of the decent ones.

Her face tilted up, and his knees nearly buckled at the need that turned the clear ice blue of her eyes into opaque azure pools. She wanted this as badly as he did.

"I don't usually do this," she whispered in a shaky voice that punched him in the place deep inside that made him male.

"I don't either," he whispered back.

"I...I can't get pregnant," she said softly. "Not until I absorb an azurite."

He had no idea what the hell she was talking about, but it didn't matter. Fertility had been one of the things taken from him when his wings were bound. No illegal half-demon babies for him.

Dying to taste her—and to get away from an incredibly uncomfortable subject—he lowered his mouth to hers.

He'd intended the kiss to be gentle. Exploratory. But she wasn't having any of that.

Throwing her arms around him, she deepened the kiss, her tongue meeting his in a violent clash. Her legs came up and wrapped around his hips, and he hissed at the feel of her warm center grinding against his hard length. She undulated wildly, her firm breasts pressing against the hard wall of his chest. Man, she felt good. So good he had to slide a hand between their bodies to reduce the friction that was threatening to ruin this whole thing.

She moaned at the contact of his fingers on her core, so he pressed against the fabric of her leggings, letting his touch both soothe and inflame. The scent of her arousal stoked his, making him crazy, making him want more.

Now.

He spun her against the wall and, using only his severely reduced angelic powers, he lifted her up next to a painting of loose rubies and a pearl necklace spilling out of a gold chalice. The surprise in her eyes turned hot as she hung there, exposed to his gaze and his mercy. With his hands free and her body pinned so she could barely squirm, he peeled off her leggings, leaving her only in her silk shirt and bright aquamarine lace underwear.

Stunning.

His mouth watered as he skimmed his palms up her creamy thighs and hooked his thumbs under the elastic of her panties.

"Yes," she breathed, her body quivering with anticipation. "Touch me."

She said it as if he was capable of resisting. No chance of that. He'd love to take the time to tease her, to make her beg, but he was like a man who had been wandering in a scorching desert for days and who had just come upon an oasis.

Greedily, he pushed one thumb between her folds and stroked her silky moisture through her slit, circling her swollen nub before dropping lower to penetrate her deeply. She threw her head back and arched into his hand as much as the angelic hold on her would allow.

Damn, she was beautiful, her hair whipping around her face as she tossed her head, her cheeks glowing with a rosy tinge that matched the color of her tongue as she held it between her clenched teeth.

Eager for more, he tugged off her panties, careful to not tear them when they caught around her ankles. As he straightened, he kissed and licked his way up her leg, savoring her smooth skin and every little catch of her breath. His own breathing was labored, his heartbeat hammering inside his rib cage as if urging him on. Not one to ignore the signals his body was sending him, he flicked his tongue over the swollen hills of Jedda's sex. At her cry of ecstasy, he dipped his tongue into her slick valley, making her cry out again and making his cock jerk with the first stirrings of orgasm. He didn't want this to end, wanted to lick her until she begged him to stop, but it had been a long time since he'd been with a female, and his body was humiliatingly ready to go off.

With a snarl of both regret and anticipation, he roughly parted her thighs and entered her in one smooth motion. His power still held her against the wall, so he planted his forearms next to her head and steadied himself as he surged against her.

"Razriel," she moaned, jolting him out of his lust with the use of his angel name, but only until she locked her legs around his waist and arched, taking him so deep he didn't think they'd ever come untangled.

His blood pumped like he was in battle, adrenaline searing his veins and skin until every part of him felt more alive than he'd been in years. Decades. His balls throbbed and tightened, and panting, he pounded into her, her delicate whimpers mingling with his groans of pleasure.

She came with no warning, stiffening against him, a muffled shout tearing from her throat. Her silken sheath squeezed him, catapulting him into his own electric explosion of ecstasy that made him see colors that put her hyper-bright room and clothes to shame.

As they came down, he realized he'd released the power that held her against the wall, and now she clung to him so tightly that not even a drop of perspiration could get between them.

Damn, that had been good.

"You know," she murmured into his neck, "you never told me why you tracked me down at the conference and what it is you wanted me to find for you."

This probably wasn't the time to show his hand, but he didn't have to bluff, either. "Must be something in the air," he said, pulling back just enough to gauge her response in her expression, "because I actually want what Shrike wants."

She stiffened against him, and panic flared in her eyes. "I don't understand."

"The gems," he said. "The remaining two Gems of Enoch. I want them, and I believe you're the key."

# Chapter Eight

It was all Jedda could do to not erupt in a full-blown panic attack. And gem elf panic attacks were messy. Sort of an explosion of fine diamond dust poofing all around her in a massive, choking cloud. And that shit got everywhere and into everything. The last time she'd had a panic attack, the abrasive particles had clogged her vacuum cleaner's air filter and scratched her glass coffee table.

Slowly, so she wouldn't arouse suspicion, she lowered her stiff legs, allowing Razr to slip from her body.

He was still hard. Could he go again? Because she could. Over and over.

Damn, that was the best sex she'd had since...well, ever, the intensity and abruptness making it all the more intoxicating. His complete dominance of her, immobilizing her so she was helpless to do anything but surrender to his touch, had been unexpected, exciting, and something her human partners had never done.

She was still a little dizzy as she pushed away from him and grabbed a silk robe from the closet. Peridot green, of course.

"Look," she said, sounding like she'd just gotten up after a wild night of partying and not enough sleep, "I don't know why these gemstones are suddenly on the radar, but you heard me tell Shrike that I can't find them. And even if I could find them, I'd have to give them to him or that Lothar curse is going to make my life a living hell."

Gods, what was she going to do? Breaking the curse, if it was even possible, would buy her some time, but given that Shrike had sent a goon to watch her, she didn't think she'd get *that* much more time.

And really, why were the stones in demand after decades of obscurity? Both her gem and Reina's were safely ensconced in the most secure vault in the universe, and it wasn't like the dhampires gave tours of the facility for people to see what was inside. *She* couldn't even get inside, and she was a client.

Something must have happened with her sister. But what? Was she in trouble? Had she told someone about the gems?

Was she dead?

An ache of despair centered in her gut at the thought, but no, she'd have felt her sister die, just as she'd felt it when Manda took her last breath. But still, something might be terribly wrong.

Razr watched her, his thickly-muscled body still bare, his skin coated in a fine sheen of sweat, his impressive length glistening with her arousal. Even though she'd just had the most amazing orgasm ever, she still felt a swell of desire expand between her legs, diminished only by the sobering subject at hand.

Two fallen angels wanted the one thing she couldn't give up.

Razr scrubbed a hand over his face as if trying to scour away the disappointment in his expression. "We'll figure something out. Shrike is an overconfident douchebag, and I have faith that you can produce at least one of the gems." He gestured to the bathroom. "Mind if I use your shower?"

Relieved to put this off, even for just half an hour, she nodded. "Towels are in the cupboard by the sink, and there are some travel-sized toiletries like toothbrushes and soaps in the drawer beneath the towels. There's a steam feature in the shower too—might help if your back still hurts. Take your time." Hopefully he'd take a lot of time, because she needed to figure a way out of this mess. "I'll make some lunch if you're hungry."

His naughty smile nearly made her already shaky knees threaten to collapse. "I'm starving," he said in a low, husky voice. "That little taste of you wasn't nearly enough."

When he turned to walk away from her, the flex of the muscles in his ass and legs pushed her over the edge, and she sank into the bedside chair to collect herself for a moment. How could she be so attracted to someone she barely knew, at a time when her life was in danger?

Groaning, she buried her face in her hands. What the hell had she done? How much trouble was she in? One fallen angel seemed bent on torturing her until she gave him what he wanted, and the other seemed determined to seduce her into giving him what he wanted.

Not that she could. But what a way to go.

She wallowed in self-pity until she heard the water turn on, and then she went to the guest bathroom to clean up and dress in an azure sweatshirt and jeans before checking to see if Shrike's minion was still outside. He was, but he was smart enough to be hanging out on the other side of the street. People walked past him as if he wasn't there, and she figured he was using whatever trick it was some demons used to make themselves invisible or unnoticeable to humans.

Shit, she was screwed.

Muttering obscenities in both English and Elvish, she threw together a quick version of her favorite shepherd's pie recipe and Yorkshire puddings. Although Jedda had grown up in France, her mother had been a fan of British food, and Jedda liked to recreate her mother's dishes now and then, even if she had to eat them all by herself.

Sometimes she invited her employees to dinner, six humans whom she considered friends but who didn't know the truth about her. But for the most part, when she cooked she did so for herself.

While she prepared the meal, she considered her options. She had to look for the crystal horn Shrike wanted, for sure. But clearly, she couldn't give up the gem that had become part of her body and soul. She wouldn't give up her sister or her stone, either.

She did, however, need to find Reina.

As the food cooked, filling her flat with the savory, warm scent of beef, she peeked out the window again. Ooh, new goon. Shift change, she supposed.

"Something interesting out there?" Razr's deep voice, coming from down the hall, made her shiver.

"Not interesting," she said as he stepped up next to her, dressed in his clothes from last night. The male could definitely fill out a suit. "Annoying. Shrike sent some creep to keep an eye on me."

Razr yanked the curtain aside with a growl. Menace billowed off him, and for a moment she thought he'd go right through the window. "Stay here."

"What?" She tried to stop him as he threw open the front door. "No, wait!"

He didn't stop until he was nose to nose with the demon across the street. She couldn't hear the conversation, but she could see it getting heated, with Razr backing the guy up against a light post. A few seconds later, the demon scurried away in the direction of the nearest Harrowgate.

"What did you say to him?" she asked when Razr came back inside.

"I introduced him to a few of my friends."

She frowned. "What friends? I didn't see anyone."

It was his turn to frown at her. "You didn't see the *griminions*?"

The oven timer went off, and she started toward the kitchen. "What are *griminions*?"

"Seriously?" His heavy footsteps followed behind her. "I mean, I know not every demon knows what a *griminion* is, but you didn't even *see* them? Creepy little short dudes in robes? Glowing eyes, claws for hands..."—he held his hand at just below groin level— "...about yea high?"

"I told you, I'm not a demon. And no, I did not see any *griminions*, and from the sound of them, I'm glad I didn't." She eyed him askance. "You say they're your friends?"

"Well, not friends, exactly. More like coworkers. They were in the area."

She was about to ask what their job was and who Razr worked for when the oven timer went off again and the phone rang simultaneously. "Do you mind getting the food out of the oven while I get the phone? I'll just be a minute."

It was Sylvia from her shop with a question regarding the pricing of a couple of rare stones from Australia. By the time Jedda worked out the kinks and got off the phone, Razr had set the table and dished up.

"This looks amazing," he said as they dug in. After a bite, he made a sound of ecstasy that had her remembering what they'd done in the bedroom. "It *is* amazing."

"It's nothing special." She shrugged, outwardly nonchalant, but inside, her heart did a little happy dance at the compliment. "Do you cook?"

"Nah." He reached for a Yorkshire pudding. "I mostly eat cafeteria food."

Cafeteria food? She studied him, realizing she knew absolutely nothing about him. She'd brought him home, cared for him, slept with him, fed him...and he was a complete mystery.

If this were a movie, it would either be a fun romantic comedy or the setup for a slasher film. She swallowed dryly and got up to fetch something to drink, taking note of the knives next to the stove. As if they'd be any help if he decided to chop her up. The weapons he wore on his body made a mockery of her little cooking knives.

Not to mention that he was a fallen angel, probably capable of melting her in her socks.

She fetched a couple of sparkling waters from the fridge and sat down. "So why is it that you eat a lot of cafeteria food?"

Razr took a break from shoveling down shepherd's pie to unscrew the top off his bottle of water. "I live on sort of a campus. It's a training facility for a special kind of angel called Memitim." She must have looked as confused as she felt, because he added, "Memitim are basically earthbound human guardians. They have to earn their way into Heaven."

"Oh. Well, that must suck. Are you—*were* you—one of these Memitim?"

He shook his head. "I was born in Heaven, a full-fledged angel. Right now I'm helping to train the Memitim."

Jedda gave herself a moment to process that. She'd really never given the Heavenly realm much thought, and it had certainly never occurred to her that there would be more than one kind of angel, let alone earthbound ones.

"You know, you're not what I would have expected from a fallen angel."

He paused with the mouth of the water bottle near his lips. "Yeah? What did you expect?"

"Shrike." She spread her napkin in her lap. "I mean, other than you, he's the only fallen angel I've ever met. He's what I would have expected. You don't seem as...damaged."

"I'm...not sure how to respond to that." He smiled, his charm proving her point. "I feel like I need to defend myself and insist that I'm all kinds of damaged." He tipped the bottle up, and she became mesmerized at the way his throat worked with each swallow, his supple skin rippling over straining tendons. "So," he said after he'd downed most of the bottle, "you say you're an elf."

"I *am* an elf." She tucked her hair behind one pointy ear so he couldn't miss it. *She* didn't miss the way he'd changed the subject. Now she was super curious about his damage.

His mouth quirked in amusement. "A lot of demons have pointy ears."

"I'm not a demon." How insulting. And how many times did she have to tell him that? Annoyed, she reached for her bottle of water, but in her haste, she knocked it over, striking the marble napkin holder. The bottle shattered, spilling foamy seltzer everywhere. "Dammit." She reached for a napkin, but once again her haste cost her, and she sliced her arm on a broken piece of glass.

Blood splashed on the table, and before she could mop it up, tiny emeralds, citrine, lapis, and a dozen other gemstones formed in the splatters of blood.

"That's...interesting," Razr murmured.

"It's nothing." She swiped her hand through the mess, and instantly the gems disappeared into her palm. "I'll get this cleaned up—"

"Wait." He seized her wrist and pulled her hand close. "What just happened?" Gently, he pressed a napkin against her wound, which was already healing, but was also spilling out a couple more gemstones. "What's going on, Jedda?"

At his no-nonsense tone, soft but steely, her breath burned in her throat and her blood burned in her veins. Gem elves did everything they could to hide this secret. If people knew the truth about them, they'd be hunted into extinction, slaughtered for the wealth they carried within their bodies.

Jedda didn't know Razr. Didn't trust him. And yet, there was something about him that made her *want* to trust him.

"Jedda?" he prompted. "You can tell me."

"No," she rasped. "I can't." All around her, diamond dust poofed into the air, turning the kitchen into a priceless snow globe.

"Okay then." With a little cough, Razr released her, keeping the blood-soaked napkin. As he turned it over, a couple of sapphires pinged onto the tabletop. "I'll tell you what I think's going on. You sweat diamond dust and bleed precious gems, and you're worried I'll hang you by your feet and bleed you out for them. Am I right?"

He'd called it. Son of a bitch. She supposed there was no point in lying anymore, so she stared at the sparkling water as it *drip, drip, dripped* to the floor.

"My species...we don't locate priceless gems just to sell. We use them like fuel. They're what our bodies are made of. Our bones, our muscles, our organs. We can sense them. Not to toot my own horn, but that's why I'm such a successful gemologist."

He cocked an eyebrow. "Do you need different kinds of gems to survive?"

"You mean, could I live off, say, rubies, exclusively?" At his nod, she shook her head. "Every gem has a different chemical and mineral composition, and our bodies need certain types of stones for different functions. I need diamonds to cry and for the protective coating on my skin, for example."

Reaching out, he trailed a finger along her bicep, leaving behind a heated tingle. "Protective coating?"

"See how I sparkle in the right light? It's diamond dust. When I'm in a mine and my body detects deadly gasses or excessive heat, it absorbs the worst of it and lets me go deeper and stay longer than humans. Topaz gives me night vision. Stuff like that." She gestured to the large gemstones she kept all around the flat, many displayed as works of art, some just filling glass bowls, and others lying around waiting to be dusted. "They all give off their own unique, life-giving vibrations. We don't absorb them all—we surround ourselves with them too. Their energy is our fuel."

Sitting back in his chair, he appeared to contemplate what she'd told him. "Is their energy infinite? Or do you have to replace the gems when their energy is depleted?"

She reached out and spun the table's centerpiece, a crystal dish containing a mix of uncut gemstones, and watched the colors swirl in a multicolored blur. "Stones we keep around us provide infinite, but mild energy. For more intense energy and special abilities, we have to absorb the gems. The small ones are drained within a few months, and even the larger and most powerful ones can be depleted if we don't return to our realm every decade or so to recharge them. We can also hit capacity."

"Capacity?"

She nodded. "I'm so full of hematite that I can't absorb another one unless I break a bone and need more to heal."

"Are there ever any that you can't be around?"

"Oh, yes. Some are so powerful that they can have a corrupting effect on us, like a drug that never wears off." She'd seen that more times than she wanted to admit. "Of course, part of what makes us what we are is that we can't resist gemstones like that. We want them, even though we know we shouldn't actually use them. Those go into storage. At least, those of us who aren't crazy put them into storage."

There was a long pause as he stared at her with such intensity that she started to squirm. "Do you have any like that?"

"Several." She pushed a piece of carrot around on her plate, her appetite ruined by the topic. "Most of them are there because they're infused with evil, and I don't want them getting out into the world. I mean, can you imagine what would happen if someone like Shrike got hold of a lapis lazuli that could turn water into arsenic on a large scale?" She shuddered.

"You have a lapis lazuli that can do that?" Razr stood and headed into the kitchen.

"I have a lot of gems that are even worse," she sighed.

No way was she letting any of them go, and she'd paid the dhampires enough to keep the things stored for eternity. She especially didn't want them to fall into the hands of evil gem elves. Members of her species were just too self-destructive when they went evil, as Jedda knew all too well. Never again would she allow an evil gem to leave her possession.

Razr fetched the garbage and started to clean up the broken glass, refusing when she offered to help. "Okay, so you have this incredible affinity for gemstones. What makes you think you can't find the Gems of Enoch? Sounds like if anyone can, it's you."

"I can't just wish a gem into my possession," she said, because that was the truth. "In order to find an enchanted stone at a distance, it has to be in use. That's the only way it'll send out a strong enough signal. But even then, I have to be somewhere close."

He wiped up the last of the broken glass with a paper towel. "How close?"

She shrugged. "Once, a Svetnalu demon princess in northern Vietnam was using runes made from a lava beast, and I felt it from Malaysia. But that's rare. Really rare."

She and her sisters had felt the Gems of Enoch in use from twice as far away, but there was no way she was going to share that precious nugget of information.

"So you're saying you have no idea where any Enoch gems are, and you don't know how to find them."

She took intense, sudden interest in her plate so she wouldn't have to look at him. "That's what I'm saying," she mumbled.

There was a long silence, and she sensed disappointment rolling off him in a wave so strong that she swore she experienced it as well. Did she actually feel bad that she couldn't give him the diamond?

Finally, as he sat back down across from her, he broke the silence. "What if I can get you the crystal horn? We can get Shrike off your back with it. At least buy some extra time, and I'll help you find the Enoch gems."

Help her? It wouldn't make any difference. She couldn't give up her diamond. But the crystal devil's horn? Was he serious? "What about the horn? How can you help me get it? I thought you didn't know what it even was?"

"After you and Shrike described it, I realized I'd seen it before." He waggled his brows. "I just happen to know who owns one."

She rolled her eyes. "That's next to impossible. Probably a replica. I told you, according to legend there are only two—"

"And one of them happens to belong to my boss."

He really was delusional. But she played along. "Okay," she said. "I'll bite. Who is your boss?"

"I call him Azagoth, but you probably know him as the Grim Reaper."

She wasn't sure if she should laugh or laugh...harder. The Grim Reaper? Demons were always calling themselves all kinds of crazy shit. She'd met a dozen idiots who swore they were Lucifer. And a dozen more who claimed to be Jack the Ripper. Hitler. Caligula. The list went on.

"Tell you what. You prove you work for the Grim Reaper, and I'll prove I'm an elf. Deal?"

"Deal." Razr grinned, that killer one that made her ovaries clench. "Come on, Dobby. Let's go."

# Chapter Nine

*Dobby?* Jedda revised her opinion about Razr. He was clearly broken. Also? Sheoul-gra was super creepy.

Jedda had spent most of her life in the human realm, with occasional jaunts to the elven and demon realms, but the Grim Reaper's home was, by far, the most unsettling place she'd been. Razr had explained it as being a holding tank for the souls of dead demons and evil humans, but apparently there were two distinct sections. One was for the living, and the other, known as the Inner Sanctum, was where the souls were kept, presided over by a fallen angel named Hades, but not until Azagoth checked out every one of them.

At first glance upon materializing on the arrival pad, everything seemed fairly normal. A green, grassy landscape stretched forever, broken by a forest in the distance. Ancient Greek-style buildings formed a small city dotted by fountains and sculptures, all lending a peaceful vibe.

But once inside the largest of the buildings, things got bizarre, weird, and a little scary. From the room filled with tortured, twisted statues to the zany little demon things Razr called *griminions*, Azagoth's home left her wanting only to go back to *her* home.

"Why is it that I can see the *griminions* down here but not in the human realm?" she asked as one of them skittered past, chattering in some language that reminded her of the squirrels that scolded her every morning on the walk to work.

"It's probably because you're an elf. Humans can't usually see them, either."

"Oh, now you believe me?"

He cast her a sideways glance as they started down a shadowy hallway. "It's actually starting to make sense."

"Hmph." She poked him in the ribs. "I told you so."

"Don't get cocky, Keebler," he warned her, but his tone was teasing and his made-for-sin mouth was quirked in mischief. "You still haven't proved it."

Stubborn male. "Don't worry, I will." A dark, intense buzz vibrated through her, coming from a room ahead. When Razr stopped in front of it, she eyed the iron doors with curiosity. "What's in here?"

"A bunch of shit Azagoth has collected from people who owe him." Razr waved to a big guy with a blue Mohawk at the far end of the hall. "Or people he blackmailed. I don't know. In any case, it's a museum of rare and valuable crap."

She couldn't tell if he was kidding about the blackmail, but she didn't really care. She'd shoved a precious gem up a dude's ass. Who was she to judge?

"Like enchanted stones?" She bounced on her toes in excitement.

"Yeah." He grinned. "Want to see?"

"Did you really have to ask?"

The hard clack of booted feet echoed through the hallway as Razr went to open the door.

"Hey, Razr, hold up." The Mohawked guy was walking toward them, shirtless, his color-shifting pants making Jedda dizzy. A statuesque female, her shiny mink-brown hair piled in a knot on top of her head, walked a step ahead of him with the authority of a queen. She was a bright light in the gloom that surrounded them, her flirty yellow sundress flapping around her knees, her matching flip-flops snapping against her heels.

"What's up?" Razr asked.

"Azagoth wants to see you in the library. Lilliana will take care of your female."

"I'm not his female," Jedda said, hoping she didn't sound as flustered as she felt. "We're...business partners." She held out her hand. "I'm Jedda Brighton."

Mohawk stared at her hand. The female *tsked* at him and took Jedda's palm in hers. "I'm Lilliana. Azagoth is my husband." She jacked her thumb at the Mowawked guy. "That's Hades. He sometimes forgets basic manners."

"Don't need 'em where I live."

Razr snorted. "Don't believe him. His mate keeps him in line."

"Pfft." Hades waved his hand in dismissal. "She knows who rules the roost."

Lilliana laughed. "Cat does."

Hades's shoulders slumped. "Yeah." Suddenly, he grinned and waggled his brows. "But she has sex with me, so it's all good."

If anyone had told Jedda she'd ever be standing in front of *the* Hades, she'd have given them the same colorectal procedure she'd performed on Tom the Walking Whisky Dick. The thought made her realize she could use a drink, and she really wasn't even a fan of alcohol.

"Come on, asshole." Hades clapped Razr on the shoulder and started him down the hall, leaving her alone with a complete stranger. In a strange place. Full of strange things.

She was going to start poofing diamond dust at any moment.

"Don't worry, Jedda," Razr called back from over his shoulder. His gaze bored into her, assuring her with a look that he meant what he was saying. "You're safe here. I promise."

Was it crazy that she believed him? Someone she'd just met? Probably, but she'd never encountered anyone whose energy synced so well with hers. It was as if he was somehow reaching inside her and holding her life-stone's essence, streaming directly from the Enoch diamond, in his palm. Was this what love felt like? Was she as crazy to think that as she was to believe in him?

"Would you like a tour?" Lilliana asked, thankfully interrupting Jedda's insane thoughts. "The boys could be a while. Razr will find us when he's done."

Jedda agreed, not having anything else to do. Besides, she was curious. This was a once-in-a-lifetime opportunity, and she might even discover some new gemstones in the material that made up this mysterious realm.

The tour proved to be fascinating. She and Lilliana walked through forests full of animals from the human realm, and they watched dozens of Memitim angels spar and play team sports. Apparently, the team sports were Razr's idea to develop their teamwork skills. Lilliana said there'd been a lot of complaining and even fights at first, but now the Memitim—who were, unbelievably, all Azagoth's children—were getting along better.

Jedda even got to meet a few Unfallen angels, which was a strange concept, and an ugly one. Apparently, Unfallen angels needed to enter Sheoul-proper in order to complete their fall and make them true fallen angels, and these people had chosen the sanctuary of Azagoth's realm to stay safe. They lived in fear of being forcibly dragged to Hell, which would destroy any chance of redemption. Jedda shuddered as she and Lilliana walked back to the main building.

"You okay?" Lilliana asked, stepping behind Jedda to usher her through the front doors.

"I'm fine. I guess I just didn't realize what Razr is going through. He must be terrified that he won't be able to get back into Heaven."

"Well," Lilliana said wryly, "Heaven isn't all it's cracked up to be."

Jedda thought about Becky, one of her dedicated church-going employees. "I know a few humans who would be very upset to hear that."

Lilliana laughed. "Humans have it pretty good in Heaven. For angels...it's all work and politics." She turned down a narrow hallway. "You hungry? I had Suzanne put out some tea and scones."

As if on cue, Jedda's stomach rumbled. "My favorite."

Lilliana led her to a small but elegant dining room, where a table with the promised refreshments had been set out. A tall brunette female wearing jeans and a skimpy black tank top entered from an arched doorway carrying a tray of finger sandwiches.

"It's all ready," the female said as she placed the tray on the table. "I know you didn't ask for the sandwiches, but I like making them."

"Suzanne likes cutting food into tinier food," Lilliana explained, a note of affection in her voice. "When it's her week of kitchen duty, everything we eat is miniature."

Suzanne jammed a fist on her hip. "If it's bite size—"

"It's the right size," Lilliana finished with a teasing roll of her eyes.

"Very funny," Suzanne muttered. "Now, if you don't mind, I'm going to go check on my human."

Jedda took a seat. "Her human?"

Lilliana poured tea into two delicate, gold-rimmed teacups shaped like human skulls. Sheoul-gra was the strangest, most disconcerting mix of normal and horrifying.

"Remember when I said Memitim are charged with guarding humans called *primori?*" Lilliana asked.

Jedda nodded, recalling Lilliana saying that *primori* were humans, and sometimes demons, who were in some way important to the fabric of existence.

"Well," Lillana continued, "Suzanne just got her first *primori*. We're very proud."

Grinning, Suzanne held out her wrist, revealing a small, round mark. "This is an *heraldi*. It represents his life. If it burns, he's in trouble. He's fine right now, but I should still check on him."

Lilliana leaned close to Jedda and said in a conspiratorial whisper, "Suzanne has a crush."

"I do not." Suzanne's cheeks flamed hot, betraying her. "But he *is* to die for. He just needs to dump the necrocrotch skank he's with."

Lilliana's smile faltered a little. "Don't get involved, Suz. You know better."

"I know, I know." Suzanne gave a cheery wave as she started toward the door, probably anxious to avoid a lecture. "Sex with humans is bad. But come on, give me some credit for necrocrotch."

"Necrocrotch?" A blond male munching on a bag of chips came out of the kitchen with another male whose long hair, a couple of shades darker, swung loosely around his shoulders. Both were dressed in leather, their chests, waists, and hips slung with weapons. "Sweet. I'm totally borrowing that."

Lilliana gestured to the two males. "The mouthy one is Suzanne's full brother and mentor, Hawkyn. The Fabio wannabe is Cipher. He's Unfallen."

"I call them the Unholy Alliance," Suzanne chirped affectionately.

Cipher frowned. "Who's Fabio?"

"He's a cover model from the—" Lilliana cut off as Cipher puffed up like a rooster.

"Cover model? Fuck, yeah, I could do that."

Hawkyn punched his buddy in the shoulder, and they squabbled good-naturedly as they left, leaving Jedda to marvel at the moment of normalcy in this incredibly bizarre place. She would never have guessed that people who lived in an underworld purgatory could be so...well, happy.

"I'm outta here, too," Suzanne said. "My *primori* is waiting."

"Just be careful," Lilliana called out, but all she got for her effort was a flip of the middle finger as Suzanne disappeared around the corner.

"Suzanne seems like an odd name for an angel," Jedda mused as she stared after the Memitim.

"Memitim are raised by humans, so they usually have common human names representative of the time period and region in which they were raised. Suzanne is relatively young."

"Wow." Jedda shook her head as she stirred honey into her tea. "Are any of the Memitim your children?"

Even before the question was fully out of her mouth, she kicked herself for asking it. Lilliana had explained that there were scores of Memitim baby-mamas, but it had only just occurred to Jedda that Lilliana might be one of them. Or not. Either way, it could be a touchy subject.

Fortunately, Lilliana didn't appear to be bothered by the question. "Azagoth and I don't have any children yet." She dropped a cube of sugar in her tea. "This is our time, and we're enjoying it."

Wow. Jedda hadn't spent a lot of time around demons or in the demon realm, but most of what she'd experienced when it came to demons was pure chaos. These people were focused, smart, and genuine. Reaching for a sandwich, she shook her head in amazement.

Lilliana's mouth quirked. "What is it? You look surprised about something."

"It's just that I expected the Grim Reaper's realm to be...well, not this."

"You expected torture and misery and a whole lot of scary."

Bingo. "I didn't want to say it out loud, but yes."

The other woman blew steam off the surface of her tea. "That's how it used to be. When I got here, in fact." She took a sip, and then she put the cup down with just the slightest *tink* against the plate. "Everyone's content here now, but make no mistake, this *is* a hell realm. This is where demon souls and the souls of evil humans are stored. And my mate can be as evil as anything you've seen."

Jedda swallowed a bite of cucumber sandwich in a painful gulp. "Can I ask you something? Something personal?"

Lilliana shrugged. "Go for it."

"On our walk, you said you lived in Heaven and got to time-travel for a living. You gave up so much to be with Azagoth. Don't you ever resent him? Even a little?"

"Never." The fierceness in Lilliana's voice made it very clear that she meant it. "I mean, I get mad at him because he can be a major asshat sometimes, but I knew what I was getting into. I make him happy, and he makes me just as happy. I'd sacrifice anything to keep it that way."

Scuffling noises from out in the hall drew Jedda's attention. Hades was striding toward them with a bloody body in his arms, and it took her a second to realize who it was. When she did, her heart skidded to a painful halt.

"Razr." Terror welled in her chest as she jumped up and darted out into the corridor. Her foot slipped in blood and she nearly went down, but she caught herself on the wall just before she crashed spectacularly. "What happened?"

Lilliana grabbed her arm from behind and pulled her around, preventing her from chasing after. "His punishment. He must have gotten the signal during his meeting with Azagoth."

"I hate that," Jedda yelled. Adrenaline coursed through her body like a billion tiny, uncut diamonds that abraded every nerve and made her tremble with rage and helplessness. She knew Razr's condition wasn't Lilliana's fault. It wasn't anyone's fault who lived down here. But it was sick and twisted, and what kind of whack job devised such cruelty anyway? "It's bullshit, and dammit, I want to help him. Right fucking now!"

Lilliana inclined her head as if she knew exactly what Jedda was going through. It didn't even make any sense. Jedda didn't know Razr that well. But she couldn't fight the pull to him, the one that made her crave him and want to care for him. To watch over him when he couldn't do it himself. She'd always been a bit of a nurturer, but she'd also been a loner, not needing anyone but herself for survival or even company.

But Razr had challenged everything she'd ever known about herself. Everything she'd ever been.

"Please," Jedda said more calmly. "Take me to him."

Lilliana didn't argue. In a matter of minutes, Jedda was inside Razr's small flat in what Lilliana had called the "instructors' dorm," patching him up the way she had at her own place. Other than a few hisses and groans when she'd cleaned his wounds, he'd been silent...but awake. His eyes, dulled by pain, had locked with hers now and then, and each time, she'd had to blink back tears.

He finally passed out, and she climbed into bed beside him, wondering where they went from here.

* * * *

Jedda woke to the prod of a very impressive erection against her hip. Smiling, she stretched, letting her body slide against Razr's as he spooned her from behind.

"You awake?" he whispered into her hair. She shivered at the feel of his warm breath fanning the back of her neck like a slow caress.

In answer, she reached back and slid her hand between their bodies to grasp his cock. He gasped, arching into her palm. He was so hot, so hard, steel and satin and a drop of silken moisture. Gently, she slid her grip from the broad head to the thick base and back up, letting her fingers memorize every bump, every ridge, every smooth plane. Each stroke made him churn his hips as he nuzzled her neck and dropped his arm around her to cup her breast.

Oh, yes. This was what she'd missed when they'd had sex the other day. Not that she was complaining, but to be able to touch, to play... The decadence of it made her entire body go liquid with desire.

He pinched her nipple and rolled it between his thumb and finger, tweaking it until it was so sensitive it felt like it was directly connected to her core. An orgasm hovered between her thighs and they'd barely gotten started.

"Jedda..." His voice was so tortured, so...male, and she went utterly wet.

Twisting, she looked over her shoulder at him, and in the glow of the nightlight from the bathroom, he was incredible. Passion and raw hunger lurked in his half-lidded eyes, his full lips parted on panting breaths, and she suddenly wanted that mouth on her body. Tasting her. Licking her. Kissing her. Didn't matter.

As if he could read her mind, he reached over and caught her chin in his hand to tilt her face toward his. As he captured her mouth, he flipped her onto her knees so they were upright, her back against his chest, his erection cradled in the seam of her ass, and his other hand playing between her legs. He was rough with her, like before in her bedroom, his tongue thrusting in her mouth, his finger thrusting in her core.

Her body jerked wildly, chasing what only he could give her.

"I don't know why I want you so badly," he murmured as he tore his mouth away from hers to kiss a blazing path down her neck. "You're just so...damned...beautiful. Every time I look at you, I want to be inside you."

Now she'd wonder what he was thinking whenever he looked her way, and she loved it. Half-crazed by his words, she angled her pelvis to give him better access and cried out as his other hand joined the first, one fucking her with fingers, the other tweaking her clit.

"You're so wet," he murmured. "You're going to drench me when you come..."

Pleasure ripped through her, and she came in an explosive blast that took her by surprise and threw her right out of her ever-loving mind. She barely noticed how he bent her forward roughly, urgently, and entered her in a powerful, dominating thrust that banged the headboard into the wall.

She came again before he was fully seated inside her, her walls pulsating around him, grabbing him.

He ground his hips into her, cursing, shouting, his fingers scoring her hips.

Bucking against him, she begged for more, *demanded* more, and he gave it to her. Lifting her hips so her knees came off the mattress and limited her control, he drove into her with powerful thrusts, shoving her toward the headboard with every slap of his thighs against hers. Pressure built as each wild stroke of molten friction reduced her to a mass of quivering need.

She screamed into the pillow as the stinging heat of release tore at her again. His primal shouts joined hers, and his hot jets filled her even as her breath left her.

As she collapsed onto the mattress, him on top of her, all she could think was that he was as perfect and rare and special as an expertly cut, flawless diamond. A girl's best friend, for sure.

How many girls had considered him a flawless diamond?

Not that it mattered, she supposed, but still, the thought might as well have been a cold shower.

"Hey." He shifted his weight, rolling onto his side but keeping one hand on her back, massaging gently. "You okay?"

How had he known? "Yeah." She smiled and turned over. "I'm just wondering what we're doing." Her face heated as she glanced at his fabulously naked body. "I mean, besides the obvious."

With a heavy sigh, he flopped onto his back and stared at the wood beams in the ceiling. "I don't know. I didn't expect to be so...enamored of you."

"Enamored?" She grinned, basking in the compliment. But something about the way he said he hadn't *expected* to be enamored with her left her unsettled. Maybe it was nothing. But what *had* he expected? And why had he had any expectations of a stranger at all?

"Enamored," he agreed, but he didn't sound too happy about it, leaving her with even more misgivings. "It's strange because I only needed one thing from you...and this wasn't it." He turned to her, his gaze locking with hers with such intensity that it stole her breath. "You've taken care of me when you didn't need to. You protected me from Shrike when you didn't have to. You even fed me and trusted me to bring you here. Why?"

"I don't know," she admitted. "I usually avoid your type, but I was just...drawn to you, I guess."

Plus, if she was going to get out from under Shrike's dinner party curse, she needed help, and Razr had offered. Granted, it might only be because he wanted her to "find" the two remaining Gems of Enoch, but still. She didn't have any other allies at this point, one of the downsides of only having human friends.

"My type?"

"Otherworldly," she explained. "Demons, shapeshifters, weres, angels, fallen angels."

He leveled an are-you-kidding look at her. "Ah, I hate to break it to you, but you're an otherworlder too."

"Elves don't consider themselves part of your world. We identify more with humans. More of us live in the human world than in the elven one, in fact."

"Why is that?"

Faintly, from somewhere outside, she heard a whistle and someone yell, "Foul!" The Memitim playing some sort of sport, she guessed.

"The elven realm is kind of...unreal. It's like living in a medieval dream." She reconsidered that. "Well, a clean, cheery medieval dream."

Razr gasped in mock horror. "Sounds awful. I can see why you guys would rather live in the human realm."

She laughed, enjoying this exploratory time with him. It was easy to talk to him, something she'd never been able to do with her human lovers. "What's your favorite food?"

"What does that have to do with life in...what? Middle Earth? Shannara? I don't know...Pandora?"

Torn between annoyance and amusement, she settled for shaking her head in exasperation. "Just tell me your favorite food. Maybe a dessert. Also, Pandora doesn't have any elves."

"The Na'vi have pointed ears," he shot back with a playful grin that tugged at her heart. "And salted caramel pie."

That did sound tasty. "Well, imagine your diet consisted of only salted caramel pie. That's it. Every day. And imagine having nothing to do but look for gemstones. Everything around you is perfect and bright and people rarely even argue." Mostly, elves just vacationed in their realm or lived like American snowbirds, people who summered in a northern state and wintered in a southern one. "It's nice to visit and recharge, but peace is tedious, and living in the chaos of the human world is, in its own way, more rewarding."

His expression turned contemplative. Maybe a little sad, and she wanted to hug him.

"I get that," he said softly. "Heaven is kind of like that. People argue—angels are hotheads—but for any kind of real challenge or entertainment, you have to get out of there." He smirked, and her heart tugged again, harder. She loved the playful side of him. "That's why I know about Pandora and Dobby and Shannara. Humans might be inferior creatures, but man, they know how to tell a story." Reaching out, he trailed a finger around the shell of her ear, and she shivered with delight. "What do you tell them about your Spock ears?"

"Nothing. Their selective cognizance renders them blind to our physiology unless we point it out or they're already familiar with the otherworld."

"So...do you date humans?" He made it sound like he was asking if she dated dung beetles.

"Since I live in the human realm, humans do tend to make up the majority of the dating pool." Although she had dated a werewolf once. Just once. They were grumpy as hell.

"So that's a yes." There was an underlying note of, what...jealousy, maybe?...in his voice that both flattered and annoyed her. "Are you dating someone now?"

The annoyance turned to anger, and she levered into a sit. "I wouldn't be here if I were, and if it bothers you, maybe you should have asked before we fucked the first time." She started to swing her legs out of bed, but he captured her wrist and held her back.

"Wait. You're right. It's just that I didn't expect this to happen. I figured I'd meet you, have the gemstones within a few hours, and I'd be back in Heaven by now."

She felt like she'd been kicked in the gut. "Back in Heaven? So soon? Don't Unfallen have to save the planet or perform some great heroic act or something?" Lilliana had been pretty clear about that. It wasn't easy to get back into Heaven, and according to her, only a handful of Unfallen ever had.

He flinched. The barest twitch of his facial muscles, but it was there. "I'm not Unfallen." His voice was gruff, as if he had to force the words out, and an uneasy feeling tightened in her chest. Where was this going? "I was tossed out of Heaven and put into Azagoth's service, but I can earn my way back into Heaven if I complete my mission. I can end the torture of the *Azdai* glyph and throw away that damned cat-o'-nines I carry around. I just need the Gems of Enoch to do it, and only you can help me."

It was her turn to flinch. She couldn't help him. It was

impossible. "Surely there's another way you can earn your way back into Heaven," she said desperately. "I can help you with anything else. Anything. You name it."

"It has to be the Gems of Enoch." His voice was as rough as the floor of a mine shaft. "One of them, at least. The Ice Diamond. I need it."

"Why?" Immediately after she asked, the tightness in her chest became excruciating, and she realized she didn't want to know.

Dark shadows flitted in his eyes as he held up his hand. The ring on his finger, the one that had previously sported what she'd believed to be a black diamond, now shone with a familiar silver-blue light. His words from back at her house when she'd asked him what he'd done to get thrown out of Heaven screamed through her brain.

*"I was part of an elite demon-slaying team. We got careless one day, and our carelessness cost lives and property."*

Oh, gods. Oh, no. Oh, please, *no.*

But no amount of pleading or denial changed what, deep inside, she knew to be the truth.

"Because its loss is why my wings were bound and my powers were stripped. It's why I have to be flogged half to death and why I was kicked out of Heaven." He spoke through clenched teeth, his voice thick with emotion. "That gemstone is mine, and I want it back."

# Chapter Ten

Razr had fucked up. Big time.

Oh, he didn't regret telling Jedda that the stone he'd wanted her to "find" belonged to him. She'd either cop to having it or she wouldn't. What he regretted was that he'd let this get personal. He'd gotten too close to her, and the crazy thing was that he didn't even know how it happened. Or when.

All he knew was that when she'd started talking about dating humans, he suddenly wanted to find every one of her past lovers and put them in the ground while he was still considered enough of a fallen angel to get away with it.

And now his feelings were going to make shit real fucking awkward if she didn't admit to sending his Enoch gem to Scotland for safekeeping.

After dropping the truth on her like a two-ton bomb, he let her process the news. As he showered—alone—he told himself that he hadn't given her even a second to respond because he'd needed to clean up. But the truth was that he didn't want her to lie to him. He'd give her time to do the right thing on her own.

*Please do the right thing.*

His chest tightened as he considered what would happen if she did hand over the stone. He'd go back to Heaven, and she'd... Well, she'd be stuck on Earth, dating inferior human men and scouring the planet for valuable stones for evil assholes like Shrike.

Shrike. Shit. Razr was going to have to do something about that douchebag. The original plan had been to placate the guy with the crystal horn, which Azagoth had agreed to give up under one condition: That even after Razr had been restored as Razriel, he would continue training the Memitim twice a month.

For the next century. And after the century of work was up, he wanted the crystal horn back.

No, Azagoth didn't give away anything for free or out of the goodness of his black heart. The Grim Reaper put a price on everything, and he always got the better end of the bargain.

After showering, Razr turned the bathroom over to Jedda, intentionally keeping the conversation limited so they didn't have to discuss his Enoch gem. Yet. While she showered, he dressed in the only clothes besides his burlap robes he had, the faded Levi's, plain black T-shirt, leather jacket, and black boots he'd worn to Scotland. He didn't need much since he rarely left Sheoul-gra, after all.

Jedda came out of the bathroom in the outfit she'd worn here yesterday: black skinny jeans, an oversized jade button-down shirt, and leather ankle boots. Her wet hair hung in a cascade of shimmering silver-blue down her back, a few strands curling around her chin and flushed pink cheeks. Her delicately pointed ears peeked out from the curtain of hair, and if he hadn't seen the elf in her before, he did now.

Was it really true? In the library last night before his *Azdai* glyph had demanded a sound whipping, he'd asked Azagoth and Hades if they were aware of the existence of elves. Hades scoffed at the notion, but Azagoth had been less skeptical.

"I've heard tales of their realm," Azagoth had said, "supposedly shared by fairies, as well. But if they exist, their deaths aren't governed by demon law."

"Meaning you've never had an elf soul come through Sheoul-gra," Razr mused, disappointed in Azagoth's answer. He'd hoped the ancient fallen angel who seemed to know everything would have some insight into Jedda's story.

Azagoth had confirmed the fact that he'd never seen an elf soul...and then he promptly flogged the hell out of him.

Razr couldn't fucking wait to be done with this shit.

"So what now?" Jedda shifted her weight with uncharacteristic nervousness as he finished tying his boots. She had to be wondering what to tell him about the diamond. She might even be wondering if he knew she had it.

"Now we grab the crystal horn and get a bite to eat. We can plot our next move over breakfast." Hopefully, *her* next move would be to tell him she had his gem, but one thing at a time.

She offered him a fragile smile. "Sounds good." She glanced over at the closet and then back at him. "Why is your closet full of robes? Is that your uniform down here?"

He went so taut that even his brain shut down for a second. He'd never told anyone about them. Not even Azagoth.

Back at Jedda's apartment, she'd mentioned that he didn't seem damaged, but those robes... Those were his damage. No, he wasn't broken and bitter like so many fallen angels, but he carried scars and remorse like everyone else, and sometimes self-flagellation was more effective than anything others could do to him.

"Razr?" She moved closer, until he could smell the pine-scented soap she'd used in his shower. "What is it? You can tell me."

"Can I?" He stood, towering over her in a move meant not to intimidate, but to make an impression. "If I tell you, will you promise to give me a straight answer when the time comes?"

She blinked, confused and caught in a trap. If she said no, she'd be admitting she had something to hide. If she said yes, she'd be obligated to tell the truth no matter what he asked.

"I...ah...of course."

He swung open his apartment door and ushered her out. His voice was mortifyingly hoarse when he spoke. "The robes aren't a uniform. I choose to wear them because they're abrasive and painful on my back when it's sensitive from the floggings, and they constantly remind me why I'm here."

Sometimes, when his guilt was extra intense, he'd actually give himself a lash or two, just so he felt more pain. But that little shameful secret was his and his alone.

He felt her eyes on him as they exited the dormitory building and walked across the lawn to Azagoth's manor.

"Doesn't being here remind you of that?"

"It isn't enough," he snapped, years of regret and anger spilling into his words. "People died because my team and I lost valuable weapons in the fight against demons." He mounted the massive staircase, his booted feet clanging loudly in the still air. "If we don't recover my diamond, the garnet, and the bracelet that goes with it, we'll be that much weaker in the Final Battle. Worse, if those stones fall into the wrong hands, they could be used for evil."

As they entered the building he glanced over at Jedda, who looked a little green. Now she *really* looked like an elf.

"I'm sorry." Her voice was ragged and her eyes haunted, and he wondered what she was thinking. What she was feeling. Guilt, maybe?

Inhaling deeply, he calmed himself, forcing the past behind him. For now.

He paused in front of the room they had been about to enter yesterday before Hades summoned him to Azagoth's library. "You're going to love it in here."

"I know." Shadows still flitted in her eyes, but her skin had brightened with excitement, glittering faintly in the light from the sconces on the walls. "I can already sense the power emanating from at least a dozen gemstones."

He threw open the door, and she didn't wait. She was practically a blur as she raced around the room, stopping in front of various display cases and stands. Some things she touched, some she avoided, and when she saw the crystal horn she both smiled and backed away, muttering something about quartz crystal and kryptonite. She reminded him of a delicate hummingbird, flitting from treasure to treasure, and when she finally came to rest at a brilliant ruby the size of her fist, he joined her.

"This one practically vibrates with power," she whispered. "It's so evil, but so...tempting."

He remembered what she'd said about some stones acting like drugs on her species, and he wondered if she was falling under the ruby's intoxicating spell.

"That," he said, as he peered at the gemstone from over her shoulder, "was given to Azagoth by Lucifer himself."

She jerked back with a hiss. "Satan?"

He was close enough to feel her heat and smell her natural, spicy scent beneath the artificial pine of his soap, and his cock stirred to life again. Not that he could do anything about it here, in Azagoth's plunder room. Disrespecting the Grim Reaper landed you in the statue room as a living work of grotesque art.

"Satan and Lucifer are two different people," he told her. "Lucifer is dead, but some say his spirit lives on in that stone." It wasn't true—Azagoth would know if that were the case. But it was hard to kill rumors like that.

And sometimes, you didn't want to kill them. You wanted to encourage them.

"So much malevolence in that one." Jedda shuddered and moved on to the slightly smaller blue topaz next to the ruby. "This one, too. My sister Manda would have loved it." She turned to him, her expression troubled, her crystal eyes glassier than usual. "Don't let Azagoth trade these, or sell them, or give them away. They're dangerous." She swallowed. "Really dangerous."

"I don't have much influence over him, but I'll tell him what you said."

She nodded absently and moved on to the next gem, a grape-sized tanzanite that sparkled atop its black velvet base. Closing her eyes, she trailed her finger over the shiny surface. "This one is incredibly powerful. Full of neutral energy. So much that an elf could absorb it, but the stone itself would have to be warehoused."

He stared at her, confused. "Wait. When you absorb gemstones, don't they disappear into your body?"

"Ideally, yes." As she spoke she looked down at the tanzanite, her long lashes casting shadows on her face. She was mesmerized by the gem, but he was mesmerized by what she was saying, unsure if he liked where this might be going. "But some stones are too large or too strong to be fully contained in our bodies. We can absorb their properties, but the stone itself must be stored somewhere safe."

He froze as the implications of what she'd just said sunk in. If she'd absorbed his Enoch gem, it could be lost to him. "Somewhere safe," he repeated, almost numbly. "Like a dhampire vault protected by Wardens?"

"Exactly," she said with a nod, and ice formed in his chest. "The stones need to be protected because if one were to fall into the wrong hands, it could destroy us." Her gaze flew up as if she sensed his mood, and she laid an apprehensive hand on his arm. Her touch was gentle, her voice concerned, and he wasn't ready for any of it. He stepped away. She followed. "Razr? What's wrong?"

"What's wrong?" he rasped. "What's *wrong*? I saw the Enoch

diamond in Scotland. *My* diamond. And I'm thinking I might not be getting it back."

"What?" Her head snapped back as if he'd slapped her, shock written all over her face. But on its heels was anger, coming in fast and hot. "Wait." She advanced on him, finger pointed like a weapon. "You've known all along that I had it? You've been lying to me this whole time? Why the charade?"

"Because I didn't know you," he said. "I didn't know what you do with the gems. And it was too important to fuck up. I thought you were just storing it, but... You absorbed it, didn't you?" It was part of her. He knew it. That was why, at Shrike's castle, his ring connected to her like it was linking to Wi-Fi.

Silence stretched, the room growing so quiet that Razr heard his own heartbeat pounding in his ears. Jedda took a step back, and he smelled fear in the air. Dammit, he hadn't wanted it to go this way. And he still had questions. Lots of them.

"Jedda?"

"Yes," she whispered. "It's..." She swallowed hard and took another step back, her gaze locked on the floor. "It's my life-stone."

"Life-stone?" He didn't like the sound of that. Sounded...permanent. "What is that?"

She scooched to the side, edging toward the door. Reaching out with his mind, he locked it.

"It's my life. It's the building block on which all the other stones sit. Only my death will release it." A cloud of diamond dust formed around her, glittering in the overhead lights, coating the artifacts nearby.

Fuck. This just kept getting worse. "Can you replace it? Obviously you survived before you got it, right?"

It wasn't cold in here, but she shivered and wrapped her arms around herself. And she still inched toward the door. He hated that she was so afraid of him, but hell, if someone wanted the one thing that kept him alive, he'd be a little nervous, too.

"A replacement for the Enoch gem wouldn't be easy. It would have to be a stone at least as powerful as the Ice Diamond." She gestured to Azagoth's jewels. "Not even these would do. Well, maybe the Lucifer ruby, but it would turn me so evil I'd have to be destroyed." She swallowed so hard that the sound echoed around the room. "And even if I found a gem that would work, removing the energy the Enoch gem gives me would be dangerous. I'd have to be bled out and mutilated almost to the point of death. I'm sorry," she whispered.

He cursed, long and hard. "So what you're saying is that if I want my gem, you have to either be tortured or killed."

Her gaze snapped up to his, and more dust billowed out of her. "Yes," she croaked.

Mother. Fuck. He couldn't kill her. That just wasn't an option. But he was going to kill *the fuck* out of whoever stole the thing and gave it to her.

"Where did you get it?" When she didn't reply, he felt the first stirrings of unease. "Jedda," he prompted again, "where did you get the gem?"

"Don't," she begged him. "Please..."

Oh, shit. *No.* Son of a bitch, this couldn't be. The unease veered sharply to dread, the same gut-twisting, heart-pounding sensation he'd felt when he'd sensed something wrong with the custodians of the gems but hadn't found them yet.

"We had a deal," he ground out. "I tell you about my robes, you tell me whatever I want to know." That wasn't exactly the deal, but he doubted she'd quibble over it. Not now. But he wished she would. He wanted desperately for her to have a solid reason to not tell him what he feared the most—that she had taken the gems in the first place.

It made sense. The gems had been in use at the time, one turning all demons in a mile radius to ash, one healing all injured angels within a ten-mile radius, and one creating a barrier through which no demons could pass to reach the humans who stood at the center of a fifty-foot circle with the gems. He, Darlah, and Ebel had been miles away, using the harnessed gem power to devastating effect on hordes of advancing demons. He'd never been able to figure out how demons had broken through the barrier, but now he knew.

Demons *hadn't* broken through. An elf had.

Jedda started inching toward the door again, but this time he didn't feel bad for her fear. Some vengeful part of him welcomed it, and whatever shame he felt for that was drowned out by the memories of the screaming custodians.

"Tell me!"

Jedda jumped. "I...my sisters and I...we found the gems. In a cave—"

"Bullshit!" The obvious lie broke his last tenuous thread of control, and with a roar, he seized her by the throat and backed her against a display case full of weapons from the Great Demonic War of Talas. "You stole them. You killed the humans who held them and you *stole them.*"

"No!" Clawing at his arm as he held it at her throat, she shook her head wildly. "Just the one human. My sister killed her. My other sister and I, we stole the gems from the other two humans and ran. They were alive when we left them."

Fury and hurt blurred his vision, so he got right up in her face. "They died right after," he snarled. "Their lives were bound to the gems and to us. When the gems were stolen, they died. Slowly. Their organs dissolved and their bones broke, and they collapsed in on themselves. Took hours."

He trembled with the force of his rage and the horror of the memories. The human who had been bonded to Razr's gem, a young man named Nabebe, had been chosen by Razr, rescued from certain death as a baby abandoned in the streets of eighteenth-century Baghdad. Razr had raised him, trained him, and given him eternal life as long as he was in possession of the gem.

Razr's voice broke as he told Jedda exactly what had happened to the boy he'd considered a son.

"Nabebe screamed until his throat was raw and he drowned in his own blood, and *I couldn't stop it.*" All Razr had been able to do was hold the boy and vow to inflict the same punishment on the people responsible.

"Oh, gods," she croaked. "I'm sorry. I didn't know. I assumed only elves bond with gems. I mean, humans are...humans." She stopped fighting him, tears welling in her eyes, but it didn't move him at all. "It was a long time ago—"

"And that makes it okay?" he asked, incredulous.

"No, just listen. We...my sisters and I... Things were different back then." She reached up, attempting to peel his fingers away from her throat again. He loosened his grip, but right now he wanted to keep her where she was, where he could feel the beat of her heart in the palm of his hand. "Gem elves' moral alignment comes from the gems we absorb. Gemstones from the human realm are mostly neutral, and gems from the demon realm are usually tainted by evil. Then there are enchanted stones. The most powerful stone we absorb becomes our life-stone, the one we will die without. It also determines our alignment." She swallowed and licked her lips, as if needing time to collect her words. And her breath. "See, when gem elves are born, the parents have gems standing by, ready to infuse the infants within moments of birth."

He released his grip a little more, and she relaxed slightly, the heated flush in her cheeks turning mottled. "Neutral gems?"

"Not always. Obviously, the parents' alignments play a role, but so does the sibling factor." She cleared her throat. "Now, do you want to hear the rest? Because it's easier to talk when someone isn't threatening to kill me."

That was probably true.

"I'm not going anywhere," she swore. "Where would I go? I don't know how to get out of this place."

That was also probably true. Plus, the door was locked.

On top of all that, he didn't like manhandling females. And like it or not, he desperately wanted to believe she hadn't killed anyone on purpose. Which sucked, because he'd sworn to avenge Nabebe. He'd promised to slay the thieves and recover the stones and set the world right again.

Cursing, he released her and backed up, his anger receding enough that he was shamed to see the red marks his fingers had left on her pale neck.

"Thank you." She reached up and absently rubbed her throat. "So as I was telling you, gem elves are super competitive. Since we all need stones to survive, we can get really intense around them. Family members have been known to kill each other for a single, small ruby." She faltered over that, and he wondered if there was a story behind it. "When my sisters and I were born, my parents hoped to prevent us fighting over stones, so they gave us each an enchanted life-stone with unique alignments. Manda's was evil, Reina's was neutral, and mine was good."

He frowned. "Why would your parents align your newborn sister with evil?"

Her gaze drifted toward the Lucifer ruby, as if seeking its input. "Good and evil are subjective, are they not?" She smiled thinly. "In my realm, all gems and alignments are rendered neutral. Those who have absorbed evil gems can live in the elf realm and have normal lives. It's what's expected of those whose life-stones are evil. It just doesn't always work out that way." A tremor crept into her voice. "It didn't with Manda."

As strange as that sounded to Razr, he figured he didn't have much room to judge, given that some angelic traditions were just as callous and brutal. He scrubbed his hand over his jaw as he tried to put all this new information together.

"Okay, so I get the need for siblings to not fight, but how would these alignments prevent you from fighting over, say, some lady's non-enchanted diamond wedding ring?"

"Non-enchanted gemstones are common, so there's really no competition except for rare types like Taaffeite. But when it comes to enchanted gems, the alignment of our life-stone makes us crave gems of the same, or similar, alignment. Every stone outside of our alignment shifts how we feel, how we act, and it can even conflict with our life-stone and make us sick."

Interesting. And bizarre. "Can you ever change your alignment?"

"Yes. But only if we replace the life-stone, which we do a few times in our lives as we find more powerful gems. But since most of the minor gems we gather tend to match the alignment of our life-stone, if you change the alignment of your life-stone, all the gems of the old alignment will conflict with it." She glanced over at the Lucifer ruby. "Going from neutral to either good or evil isn't that risky, and even going from good or evil to neutral isn't always a disaster, but you *really* don't want to shift from evil to good or vice versa." She reached up and wound a long lock of hair around her finger. "Our life-stone also controls our hair and eye color."

"Well, shit," Razr breathed, unsure where to go from here. He hadn't exactly planned for this scenario. He especially hadn't planned to get physically involved with one of the very people he'd vowed to butcher horribly. This was extremely inconvenient. "So your sisters had the other two stones?" At her reluctant nod, he cursed. "One was found. Ebel's amethyst."

She closed her eyes and blew out a long breath. "Manda had that one. I don't know how he tracked us down, but he did. We were young and dumb, and it was before we learned to store the gems in a safe place."

She paused, and he knew that whatever she was about to say was going to mess with everything he'd always believed: that Ebel had done what was needed, and whatever he'd done was justified. But now that Razr had let Jedda into his life, his views were no longer black and white. They were now a million shades of jewel tones.

"What happened, Jedda?"

Her ice-blue eyes grew liquid, like water on the surface of a melting glacier. "He tortured us, killed Manda, and took the gem back. Reina and I barely escaped."

Irrational rage spun up at the knowledge that Ebel had tortured Jedda. Didn't matter that he'd pretty much planned to do the same thing. Which was what made the anger so irrational. Well, that and the fact that Ebel was dead, so Razr's anger was pointless.

Inhaling deeply, he cursed Ebel's name and refocused his line of questioning. "You said Manda's alignment was evil. The Gems of Enoch are good. So how was she able to absorb the stone's power without it changing her?"

"It did change her," she insisted. "But not as much as it should have. I don't know why. The gems changed all of us in different ways." She looked somewhere beyond him, somewhere in her mind he couldn't follow. "They aren't as good as you think."

That didn't make any sense. "They're infused with angel blood," he argued.

She shrugged. "I don't care if they're infused with the blood of all the archangels and Enoch himself. I'm telling you, their energy is like nothing any of us had ever felt, nothing like I've felt since. It's almost as if their frequency cycles at super-high speeds through all the alignments. We assumed they were neutral, but they're anything but."

He wasn't sure what to believe, but right now, he supposed it didn't matter. They still had a crazy fallen angel to deal with, and then he had to figure out what to do about his own situation. One thing was clear: he wasn't getting back to Heaven anytime soon.

And why didn't that bother him as much as it should?

"Razr?" Jedda's voice was small. Trembling. "Are...are you going to kill me?"

Fuck. The fact that she had to ask left him trembling as hard on the inside as she was on the outside. "No," he said, reaching for her.

With a small gasp, she shrank away from him, and he couldn't blame her. Mere moments ago, he'd yelled at her. He'd wrapped his fingers around her delicate throat. He'd terrified her.

Ashamed, he reached again, slowly, letting her come to him. It took a long time. Too long. But finally she eased into his embrace, and nothing had ever been so worth the wait.

He tucked her close, his heart breaking when she sobbed into his chest. "We'll figure something out," he swore. "We'll fix this."

How, he had no idea, and if she believed him, he deserved an Oscar.

She nodded, and then she suddenly jerked away from him. Alarmed, he instinctively looked around for an enemy, but she was actually smiling, even as a tiny diamond tear plunked to the obsidian floor.

"I have an idea. I mean, I don't know how much it'll help, but it can't hurt. Something happened recently to put the Gems of Enoch into play, right? I mean, that's why you were able to find mine in Scotland. And that's why Shrike invited me to that icky dinner party."

"Yes," he said slowly. "I've been wondering what's up with that, as well."

"Then let's grab the crystal horn and go."

"Where?"

She grinned. "Where else? Middle Earth."

# Chapter Eleven

Razr could tell that Jedda was still shaken as they materialized in the elven realm, which she'd said was known to her people as *Filneshara*, The Timeless Lands. Maybe being here on her home turf would be good for her, would ease her rattled nerves and help them both find some answers.

That was, of course, assuming they could find her sister.

"That's a pretty cool trick," he said, as the tourmaline she'd summoned for travel between elven hotspots and the The Timeless Lands disappeared back into her palm.

"Tourmaline is the only stone that allows us to travel here. We can only possess one at a time, and it can't be heavier than two ounces. Any more than that can throw us into dead space that we can't come back from."

"That sounds kind of horrible." He checked out their surroundings, disappointed that they could be anywhere in the earthly realm. They were at the top of a grassy hill surrounded by forest and meadows, which was scenic and colorful, but nothing special.

"It probably *is* horrible," she said. "No one has come back to describe the experience."

He frowned at her. "Then how do you know it exists?"

She pointed to a pond nestled in the valley of more rolling green hills in the distance. Its mirrored surface reflected sunlight from overhead and bright, candy-colored flowers in the meadows, not a single ripple marring the image.

"We can see them in the reflection sometimes. No one goes there except kids looking to scare themselves." She shook her head. "It's like when human kids play Bloody Mary with a bathroom mirror. Except this is real."

"Have you seen them?"

She shivered and started down the dirt path toward the trees. "My sisters and I went to the pond when we were girls. We saw three…I guess you could call them apparitions." She swallowed hard. "I can't imagine being trapped like that, clawing at the surface and hoping someone will save you."

Er, yeah. Razr's punishment wasn't looking so bad now.

A lavender-scented breeze rustled through the trees as they entered a jungle forest unlike anything Razr had ever seen, and the deeper into the woods they went, the more he realized he had been wrong about this realm. The trees swayed with the fragrant wind, their limbs heavy with silver-laced leaves that sprinkled glitter with every gust of air. It was clean here, with no hint of industrialization. No smog, no chemicals, no man-made filth.

As they walked, the trees got taller and more ornate, and Jedda giggled when he stumbled to a stunned halt. Mushrooms littered the forest floor, lit up like little neon bulbs in every color imaginable. Tiny winged creatures zipped between them, bouncing off their caps before darting upward in sprays of sparks. And here, in this forest, the trees grew around gemstones of every shape and size, their trunks surrounding them like string art.

"This…is extraordinary."

"Yeah," she sighed. "It is."

"Do these gemstones provide energy?"

She nodded and continued down the path. "They power everything here. Every tree grows around a gem, and each gem grows bigger with the tree. In the center of my town there's an oak growing around an emerald the size of an elephant." She pointed ahead, where the forest parted to reveal a village of buildings fashioned from live trees and thick vines, and there, at the very center, was the elephant emerald.

He couldn't stop staring in awe as she led him through the village, which bustled with activity, from people hawking baked goods or tending to gardens to a blacksmith who set a gemstone into each weapon he crafted.

"They're enchanted stones," Jedda told him as they walked past. "His weapons sell for a mint in other elf realms and Sheoul."

"There are other elf realms?"

She inclined her head in greeting at an azure-haired female who passed them with a basket of apples. "There are two, both connected to this one. The elves of those realms aren't allowed in *Filneshara* except to trade."

"Why not?"

She shrugged. "They're kind of assholes."

Man, he really needed to learn more about elves.

From somewhere above, a bird screeched, but the canopy was so thick it could have been a pterodactyl and he wouldn't have been able to identify it. No one else looked up, so he assumed it wasn't a predator, but the way the village's denizens were looking at him said he could be.

"I'm guessing you don't have a lot of visitors here. That orange-haired dude looks like he wants to put his sword between my ribs."

"The only otherworlders who come here are guests of elves." She picked up her pace, making a beeline for what appeared to be a gem show at the edge of the village. "The people here aren't afraid, just cautious. They know you have no power here."

"I don't?" Instinctively, he reached for the weak abilities he'd been left with, but it was like feeling around inside an empty box. Damn, he didn't like this. As pathetic as his remaining powers were, they'd at least been accessible. Now he felt naked. Exposed. Not even the demon realm was this disconcerting.

"Only elves wield magic here."

Angelic powers weren't "magic," but he knew what she meant. And he really, really needed to learn more about these people and this realm. He couldn't believe he hadn't known it existed. Were *any* angels aware of it?

"Jedda!" A slender male with pale pink hair and eyes waved from a booth displaying gemstones in every shade of green. "I have freshly mined jade and a cursed malachite I know you'd love." He waggled his brows, but she just laughed and waved him off.

"Not today, Tindol, but thank you."

Another elf tried to sell her a sapphire shaped like a banana, and another was convinced she'd love an ugly puke-green stone linked to a Viking legend.

"I'm just curious," Razr said as they passed yet another silver-tongued salesman. "Why do you have a gem market when you could just harvest the gemstones that grow with the trees?"

"Gods, no," Jedda gasped, her gaze darting around as if making sure no one had heard him. "That's one of the worst crimes you can commit here. No one gets away with it. No one."

One of the winged creatures he'd seen in the forest buzzed his ear, and he gently waved it away. "What happens to those who try?"

"Death by hanging."

He blinked. "I thought you said it was peaceful here."

"It is. It's not us who do the hanging." She lowered her voice and leaned close. "It's the trees."

He eyed the forest with new appreciation. "That's pretty badass."

"If you think the trees are badass, wait until you see—" She broke off and stumbled to a stop, and he instantly went on alert.

It only took a second to follow her gaze to see what had brought her up short. Just ahead, a red-haired, red-eyed female dressed in brown leather pants and a gold tunic blocked their path. A sword with a glittering ruby pommel hung at her hip, but it was the daggers she stared at Jedda that made Razr put himself between the two females.

"Tell me that's not your sister."

"I can't do that," Jedda said, her voice tight. "Razr, meet Reina."

* * * *

"Hello, Jedda."

Razr's arm snapped out to catch Jedda around the waist before she even knew her legs had wobbled. A surge of emotion flooded her, because no one had been there to catch her in a long time. His support meant even more to her given how everything had crashed down on her so hard back in Sheoul-gra. She couldn't believe she was still alive. Hell, she couldn't believe she was still alive *and* that Razr had forgiven her.

And now she was sharing her realm with him, something she'd

never shared with anyone. She just had to hope the experience wouldn't take a nasty turn.

"Reina." Jedda wasn't sure what to think or how to feel, but it was a relief to see her. She looked the same as the last time she'd seen her, with sleek garnet hair and garnet eyes that required colored contact lenses for visits to the human realm.

"I sensed your arrival," Reina said, her lips pursed in annoyance. "You haven't been here in years."

"I haven't needed to come." Jedda wanted to hug her sister, but Reina had never been comfortable with physical affection, and Jedda wasn't sure where their relationship stood anyway. "Have you been here all this time?"

Reina waved her hand dismissively, but not before Jedda caught a flash of fear in her expression, gone so fast she might have imagined it. "I've always liked it here."

Jedda gave her sister a skeptical look. "You *hate* the elven realm."

With a shrug, Reina turned to Razr, her assessing gaze a little too appreciative for Jedda's taste. "Who's this?"

There wasn't going to be an easy way to introduce Razr and explain who he was, so Jedda just blurted it out and let Reina sort it out in her own head. "His name is Razriel, and he's one of the angels we stole the Gems of Enoch from."

It took about five seconds for that to sink in, and then Reina gasped and stepped back, her face draining of color. "Surely not..."

"It's true." Razr held up his hand and wiggled his ring finger.

Reina lost more color, and a massive cloud of diamond dust exploded around her. Through the glittering cloud, a faint crimson glow outlined Reina's body, a giveaway that she was drawing on the powers of her gems to use as a weapon. And here in The Timeless Lands, elves were twice as strong as in any other realm.

"Reina, you need to calm down—"

"Why did you bring him here?" Reina rounded on Jedda. "Otaehryn herwenys es miradithas?" *What the hell were you thinking?* "Cluhurach!" *Idiot!*

"He has no power here, Reina." Jedda kept her voice calm, trying to talk her sister down. "You know that." As she'd told Razr, only elves had power in *Filneshara*, but that didn't bring back any color to Reina's face. She still eyed him like he was going to smite her where she stood.

"Why is he here?" she demanded again, her voice at a near shout that made everyone in the nearby booths stare.

"Because we have questions." She slowly moved toward her sister, casually putting herself between Reina and Razr. "The Gems of Enoch are suddenly in play, and we need to know why. Did something happen to you recently? Something that would explain the fact that two fallen angels want them when no one has bothered us since...since Manda?"

"Not recently," Reina hedged, her voice low, as if Razr couldn't hear. "Well, mostly."

"Dammit, Reina, just tell me. What's happened since the last time I saw you?"

Reina nervously smoothed her hands down the belted gold smock she wore in the elven tradition over leather pants. "I don't want to talk in front of—" She glared at Razr. "—*him*."

Razr snarled, and before Jedda could blink, he had Reina backed up against a tree. He didn't touch her. Didn't need to. His anger and size got his point across with ease.

"When you stole from me and my team, you caused irreparable damage and death. I've forgiven Jedda, but you?" He bared his teeth at her. "I don't know you, and I don't give a shit what you want. You *will* answer her questions, and you'll do it in front of me."

"We owe him that," Jedda said softly but urgently. "We owe him at least that."

"Fine." Reina slipped around Razr and moved a few feet away, twitching like an angry cat. "But you aren't going to like it."

Razr folded his arms over his chest and leaned casually against the tree he'd just backed her into. His hip hit the bright yellow topaz in the trunk's center, and he just as casually stepped away, probably remembering what the trees did to those who tried to steal the jewels.

"I already assumed as much," he said. "Start talking."

"Start talking, *please*," Reina scolded him with as much sarcasm as she could fit into three words and her voice. She made a sound of disgust and turned to Jedda. "Right after I saw you last, an angel named Darlah found me."

"Darlah." Razr went as stiff as the tree behind him. "The Enoch garnet is hers."

"Yeah, no shit," Reina snapped. "I was dating a couple of Charnel Apostles, and—"

"A couple?" Jedda shook her head. One Charnel Apostle was unbelievable. But two? Those sorcerers weren't just evil, they were nuclear-level evil. "Why?" Before the floral-scented breeze even carried away her question, she knew. Charnel Apostles could create gemstones full of powerful magic, gemstones with limited life. Basically, they were like drugs, delivering an intense boost of energy or strength or spell power for any gem elf who ingested them. Plus, they were apparently gods in bed. "Never mind. So what happened?"

"This Darlah chick found me somehow. But I was with my guys at the time, and there was a battle... Long story short, Darlah got her hand chopped off and I got her bracelet."

Razr sucked in a harsh breath. "You have it? What happened to Darlah?"

"Who the hell cares?" Reina narrowed her eyes. "Oh, wait, was she your lover?"

The heartbeat of hesitation before Razr spoke was confirmation enough for Jedda, and while she had no right to be jealous, just thinking about Razr with someone else left a bitter taste in her mouth.

"It was a long time ago," he said, catching Jedda's gaze as if to make sure she understood that. "Now, what happened to her?"

"No idea where that bitch went." Reina clacked her long nails together in irritation. "As for the bracelet, well, I *did* have it. Then I started dating this fallen angel who was climbing the political ladder in Sheoul."

Jedda's gut clenched. "Don't tell me you did what I think you did..."

Reina winced. "I did. I gave Slayte the bracelet so he could harness the garnet's power. He told me he was going to rule Sheoul. I was going to be his queen." She swiped her hair out of her face with an angry shove. "Obviously, that didn't happen." She sniffed haughtily. "Oh, and whatever you do, do *not* fuck the person wearing your gem's jewelry."

*Uh-oh.* Jedda shot a furtive glance at Razr. "Why not?"

"Because it'll bond you to them." Reina studied her nails, which were studded with peridots on top of black polish. "Found that out the hard way."

"What the fuck are you talking about?" Razr's eyes flashed, reflecting the same mix of anxiety and confusion Jedda felt. The situation with Razr had already been complicated enough.

"I mean that they can control you. You know how I can heal people with my gem? Well, apparently, my gem can also be used to tear people apart." She smoothed her top again, clearing it of imaginary wrinkles. "That bastard used me to slaughter hundreds of demons at a time. Thousands." Her voice wavered with emotion, something Jedda hadn't heard from Reina since Manda died. "It was awful, but I had these feelings for him because of the stupid bond. I *wanted* to help."

"Where is he now?" Razr asked.

"Dead. A couple of months ago."

"How?"

"You wouldn't believe me if I told you."

Razr's leather jacket creaked as he folded his arms over his chest. "Try me."

Reina sighed. "The bastard was using the power to tear through an army of demons that belonged to some guy named...Revenant, I think it was. We were in some shitty region in Sheoul, and then out of nowhere, these four psychos with hellhounds rode in on horseback like the damned Horsemen of the Apocalypse and went all kinds of crazy on him. I escaped, but not before I saw Slayte get hacked to pieces and then eaten by the hellhounds."

Ew. Jedda wished she had a soda to wash the taste of bile out of her mouth. "Where is the bracelet?"

"I don't know. Probably in a pile of hellhound shit somewhere."

"Disturbing details aside," Razr began, "that explains why the gems suddenly came onto the scene. I didn't hear about that particular battle, but the Horsemen must have told angels about it, and those angels recognized the use of the Enoch gem."

Jedda looked over at Razr. "Who are these Horsemen?"

"Reina just told you. The Four Horsemen of the Apocalypse."

Reina snorted in disbelief and Jedda laughed, but quickly sobered. He wasn't kidding. "The actual Four Horsemen? They're real? You know them?"

"They're real." He crouched to pick up what elves called "clover agates," because of their color and shape. They were pretty, but their weak energy was suitable only to nourish the tiniest of infants. "I don't know them well. I've only seen Limos and Thanatos—Famine and Death—in passing. They visit Azagoth sometimes, and they often travel with hellhounds. I don't know why. Hell, I didn't even think the beasts could be tamed."

"If those things I saw were *tamed*," Reina said, "I'd hate to see what feral hellhounds are like."

Jedda nodded in agreement. Hellhounds were some of the worst fiends she'd ever encountered. Right behind Shrike. "So is that why you're here? You're hiding from whoever has the bracelet now?"

"I'm hiding from Darlah. She swore to destroy me. I felt safe while Slayte wore the bracelet—I mean, he was a cruel psychopath, but he wouldn't let anyone hurt me. Now that he's gone..." She drew in a ragged breath. "I'm cool with hanging out here for a while." She glanced at Jedda and Razr. "So what's up with you two? How'd you end up here?"

"Long story," Jedda sighed.

Reina arched a reddish eyebrow that almost matched her hair. "You guys fucked, didn't you? Oh, man, Jedda..."

"It's okay." Jedda hoped. Shit, this was a complication she didn't need. But it also explained why she felt the way she did about Razr.

Razr must have sensed her unease because he came up next to her and took her hand. "We need to talk. Can we catch up with your sister again later?"

Reina nodded. "If you're for real and truly forgave Jedda, where does that leave me?"

"I don't know," Razr said in a quietly ominous voice, "but I give you my word that I'll protect you as much as I can. *If* you give me your word that Jedda can always locate you."

For way too long, Reina considered Razr's deal, and finally, just as Jedda began to sweat beads of sillimanite, Reina agreed. "Just know this, angel. If anything happens to Jedda, you'll never find me again. I can hide here literally forever."

Razr inclined his head in acknowledgement and then, to Jedda's surprise, Reina came over and embraced her. "Let's not lose each other again," she murmured. "Losing our parents and Manda was enough."

Jedda didn't point out that Manda was responsible for their parents' deaths—over a stupid ruby—or that Reina had defended Manda until the end. Which was why Jedda and Reina had gone their separate ways after Manda died. But maybe now was the time to put all of that to bed. Or to at least open the door for it to happen.

"Agreed," Jedda said as she pulled away. "Someday...let's talk."

Reina smiled. And then, in a gesture of goodwill, she opened her fist and offered Jedda a shiny round moonstone. Jedda's hand shook as she took it and held it in her palm. It vibrated with Reina's energy, a tracking device of sorts that would allow Jedda to locate her sister at any time, in any place.

Summoning her own moonstone took a little effort; Jedda had never been as skilled as her sisters at producing gems at will. Still, a few seconds and a few silent curse words later, she offered Reina a rough oval moonstone containing her own energy signature.

Reina took the stone, gave Jedda another hug, and disappeared inside a tree-formed archway to the elf grand hall where everyone would be gathering for supper soon.

Razr squeezed her hand, a comfort she was learning she didn't want to live without. "What was that about?"

"Healing," she said with a faint smile. "It was about healing. I think my sister is finally embracing her life-stone."

# Chapter Twelve

It was dark when Razr and Jedda arrived at her apartment. At first, the time of day didn't seem important. It wasn't until she turned on the TV that he realized they'd been gone three days.

Her eyes, which had been bright with hope when they left the elven realm, were bloodshot now, and her face seemed a little drawn, hints of shadow in the hollows under her high cheekbones. He wondered if travel between the realms took more effort than angelic travel, sort of like jet lag for humans.

With a heavy sigh, she tossed her keys into a basket filled with gemstones near the door. "I hate how time runs differently in the elven realm."

He was familiar with the concept since parts of Heaven and Sheoul operated with similar time anomalies, but he generally avoided those places. They always made him feel like he'd missed out on something, as if he'd wasted his life, and if there was one thing he'd learned in his centuries of existence, it was that every minute was precious, even for immortals. After all, immunity to natural aging didn't mean one couldn't be killed, and no matter what, everything changed. He didn't want to miss the changes.

"Okay, so." Rallying with squared shoulders and head held high, she headed to the kitchen, her long hair brushing against the swell of her fine ass with every step. He could watch that all day. "What's this bond thing Reina was talking about?"

"Ah. That." Yeah, this could get a little sticky. Repressing a groan, he scrubbed his hand over his face, partly because damn, he was tired too, and partly to buy a little time to figure out how to explain this without freaking Jedda out too much. Finally, he dropped his hands and got on with it. "The human custodians of the Gems of Enoch went through a ritual that bonded them to the gems. Then Darlah, Ebel, and I bonded ourselves to the humans."

Halting mid-step, she looked back over her shoulder at him. "You had sex with them? Isn't sex between angels and humans forbidden?"

"Ah...yeah. I mean, no. We didn't have sex with them." Well, Ebel had fallen in love with his human, but to this day Razr didn't know how intimate they'd been. "We exchanged blood. But obviously, there are a lot of ways to bond to someone."

"Can we break it?"

Razr flinched, stung. Which didn't make sense. Hers was a reasonable question. Who in their right mind would want to be tethered to someone else for life? For centuries. For all eternity, even. The idea should bother him, too.

But for some reason, he couldn't dredge up an ounce of give-a-shit. He'd been intensely attracted to Jedda before the sex, and afterward, nothing had felt different. He'd known almost from the beginning that he couldn't harm her to get his gem back, and that had nothing to do with any mystical bond. She'd been unique. Special. Decent. She'd proved as much when she'd gotten him away from Shrike and helped him recover.

She hadn't needed to do that. Truly, it hadn't been the smartest of decisions. Had he been, say, Ebel, he'd have slaughtered her without a second thought the moment he knew that doing so would release the gem.

"Razr?" Jedda turned fully around. "Can we break the bond?"

"Not while both of us are alive."

Grief swirled in her remarkable eyes, sending another spear of hurt right through him. "Well, that sucks," she muttered, and his hurt abruptly veered to anger.

"Don't worry," he snapped. "Once I tell my superiors that the two remaining Gems of Enoch are unrecoverable without destroying you and your sister and that I refuse to kill you or give up your locations, I'll probably be executed. Problem solved. The bond will be broken."

Her eyes flared in horror, making him regret his show of temper. Nabebe had taught him how easy it was to needlessly cause pain with words, a lesson he seemed to have forgotten in the years since the human's death.

"Oh, gods." Jedda closed the distance between them and laid a comforting hand on his forearm. "Are you serious? They'll kill you?"

"I don't know," he said grimly. "I don't even know if I'll tell them."

"What do you mean?" There was a desperation in her voice that called to every one of his possessive instincts, demanding that he assuage her fears, but he couldn't. All he could do was reach out and cup her cheek, telling her with a touch that, while this situation was a shit sandwich, at least they were eating it together.

And wasn't *that* all kinds of romantic? Cupid, he was not.

"I mean that I can lie indefinitely about searching for the gems," he replied. "No one has to know about you and your sister." Azagoth and Hades knew the truth about Jedda, but they wouldn't squeal. And Jim Bob knew that the Ice Diamond was in storage with the dhampires, but seeing how he wasn't exactly being upfront about who he was or what he was doing visiting Azagoth in secret, Razr doubted he was much of a threat.

"So you'd just live the way you've been living? With your wings bound and subjected to torture for the rest of your life? That's bullshit. Isn't there another way?"

He shrugged, unable to come up with any other way that made sense. "I could come clean, but that would put you at risk. Even if they don't execute me, they could take my ring and give it to another who will hunt you and your sister down." Damn, he was screwed. "No, I think it's best to never tell them. As I'm concerned, the gems are lost and will never be found."

She opened her mouth, probably to argue, but just then, the phone rang. "Hold on," she said in a stern voice that reminded him of one of his old battle coaches. "We're not done talking about this."

While she answered the phone, he considered their next move. They had to get Shrike out of the picture, both for Jedda's safety and to make sure the fallen angel's interest in the Gems of Enoch came to a permanent and, with any luck, a painful end.

Maybe if they—

He doubled over in sudden agony so intense he looked for blood and a spear wound to the gut. Clenching his teeth, he checked the back of his hand and sure enough, his *Azdai* glyph was lit up like a neon fucking sign as days' worth of pain-free time caught up with him.

"Razr?"

He heard Jedda drop the phone, and then she was there beside him, her arm around his waist as she helped steady him against the back of the couch.

"Need...to get...to Azagoth," he gritted out. "Hurry." The nearest Harrowgate was close, barely a block away, but it was going to feel like miles.

Jedda guided him to the door, effortlessly bearing his considerable weight on her diminutive frame as he leaned on her through spasms of pain. Even through the searing agony, he had to admire her strength and determination. He'd always been attracted to athletic, fighter-type females like Darlah, but he was rapidly learning that one didn't have to be big and brawny to be a warrior.

Keeping him braced against her side, one arm wrapped around him, she reached for the door with her other hand and tugged on the knob. "Oh, shit." She tugged again, this time more forcefully, but it wouldn't open.

"Is it...locked?" He felt like a jackass for asking, but sometimes the obvious got missed.

Fortunately, she didn't take offense, simply shook her head. "It doesn't feel stuck, either. More like—" She broke off with a curse. "Stay here."

As if he could do anything else. His bones felt like they were melting and taking his muscles with them. As she gently pulled away, he sagged against the wall.

She hurried to the window and let out a string of angry words in what he assumed was Elvish. He also assumed they were creative obscenities. "We're trapped."

A groan rattled his chest. "Trapped?"

"Shrike's minions. At least a dozen. They must have been watching for my return. I think they've trapped us with wards."

Every breath was labored now, as if he was breathing whips of fire. "Can you...get us to...ah, Rivendell?"

"It's Filneshara." Diamond dust filled the air, shredding his already compromised lungs, and he knew they were in real trouble. "The travel stones to my realm only work from *faeways*." Her voice was pitched with alarm, and he couldn't blame her.

But now wasn't the time to panic. As he told his Memitim students, stay active. No matter how much shit you're in, do something, anything, to stay focused.

"My pocket," he rasped. "In my pocket."

Quickly, she fumbled around in his jacket and pulled out the cat-o'-nines. Which she promptly dropped on the floor with a hiss. "You can't be serious. I can't, Razr. I can't. Please don't make me do it."

He inhaled, riding a relatively mild wave of pain as he straightened. "You have to. If we can't leave, you have to."

Her face contorted in misery. "I don't want to hurt you."

He hooked a finger under her chin, lifting her gaze to his, hating that this was hurting her. His pain didn't matter. It was hers that was tearing him apart right now. "I'm used to it. And I heal fast. You've seen it."

"I've also seen you pass out. And I saw how you looked just before you did." She turned away, her breaths coming in panicked wheezes. "I can't."

His skin was starting to blister, and inside his body, a firestorm of agony ripped through him as his bones began to fracture with audible cracks. "You can do it lightly," he said, desperately trying to keep his voice level so she wouldn't know how much this was making him want to scream.

Except that he was silent in his pain. He always had been. *Keep it inside*, his father used to say after a harsh training session. Which was all of them. One of the hazards of being born to two high-ranking, militant battle angels who expected their offspring to go down as legends, he supposed.

They'd been pretty disappointed in him, given the whole *fuck up an elite team and lose all their magic gemstones* thing. They hadn't even visited him in prison. Not once.

Jedda shook her head. Her entire body trembled and dammit, he couldn't make her do this.

"Okay," he croaked. "Get one of Shrike's guys in here." Something inside him popped, and he stumbled, catching himself on the fireplace mantel. "Hurry."

"I'm not letting some psycho stranger hurt you!"

He coughed, spewing blood. She cursed, came around him, and stripped off his shirt. She tossed it to the floor and started on his pants, which he would have enjoyed if he wasn't in agony and she wasn't about to torture him.

Something else inside him snapped—a rib, he thought, as he dropped to his knees. Shit, he was in so much pain right now that the cat in Jedda's hand would feel more like a loving stroke than a vicious rake.

She hesitated, and he had to clench his teeth to keep from screaming at her to get on with it. "Go...ahead. Do it, Jed. You can do it."

The straps came down on his back so lightly he would have laughed if he'd had the breath to do it. It hurt, but what hurt more was the cry that tore from her at the sound of the leather striking his flesh. He was so preoccupied by the misery he'd caused her that he almost didn't notice that all his other pain unrelated to the cat-o'-nine was gone now that the punishment was being executed.

He sagged in relief. "Again, Jedda. Five more." His voice was as shredded as his back was going to be.

"No," she whispered, her agony thickening the air, but a moment later she slapped the cat across his back. The blow was gentle, which somehow made it even worse. She was trying so hard not to hurt him.

"Again."

"I hate you for this," she cried out as she brought the straps down.

He hated himself, too. But it would never happen again. Once they took down Shrike, he'd take his sorry ass back to Sheoul-gra and let her have a normal life. One where she didn't have to hurt him or see him hurt.

One where he didn't have to watch her *be* hurt.

"Again, Jedda. Harder. The more painful it is, the more time I get between sessions." Usually. Sometimes the intervals were utterly random, as far as he could tell.

"No. I—"

"Do it!" he shouted. He needed her to be harsh. Make it hurt.

Give him more time. And if he had to piss her off to get it, he would. "Dammit, Jedda, fucking hit me!"

She did, a little harder. But barely. Then again. Her cry of pain tore through him, reaching all the way to his soul, and when she struck again, for the first time in his life, he screamed. Screamed not for himself and his shredded back. He screamed for her, for hurting her so deeply.

"Oh, gods, I'm so sorry," she sobbed, hitting the floor in front of him to gather him in her arms. He clutched her close as the *tink* of tiny diamond tears hitting the floor played like background music.

"No, I'm sorry," he whispered. "I am so, so sorry. Please forgive me, Jedda. *Please.*"

When she didn't say anything, he knew, and the dull ache that compressed in his chest became the most horrific torture he'd ever endured.

She didn't forgive him. But maybe that was for the best. It would make leaving her so much easier.

# Chapter Thirteen

Razr wouldn't let Jedda tend to his wounds. She'd watched him suffer, bleed, and withdraw into himself as she held him in her arms, unable to give him the one comfort he'd asked for.

Her forgiveness.

It wasn't that she didn't forgive him for making her hurt him. There was nothing *to* forgive. She'd done what she had to do, even as she hated him for it. Hated *herself* for it.

Because ultimately, it was her fault he was going through this torment in the first place.

Jedda couldn't let this go on. She couldn't let Razr live the rest of his life like this.

She had to give up his gem.

The moment they were done with Shrike—assuming they survived the meeting—she'd scour the human and demon realms for a gemstone more powerful than the Enoch gem, and if she couldn't find one, maybe Azagoth would be willing to do what needed to be done to her.

She'd die, but Razr would no longer live a life of suffering. Suffering that she was directly responsible for. If she hadn't stolen his gem, he wouldn't be in this mess.

Rain pelted the window she'd been staring out of for hours, her gaze fixed on Shrike's minions. The soaking-wet demons lurked on the sidewalk, their beady eyes as dead as she felt on the inside. On the outside, she looked the way she felt: exhausted and bruised, a result, she thought, of Shrike's Lothar curse. The last time she'd checked herself in the mirror, she'd been shocked at how gaunt she looked, and even now when she glanced down at her arms, her breath caught at the purple bruises spreading under skin that had grown dull and grayish.

She and Razr were quite the pair, weren't they?

Footsteps pounded in the hallway, and her stomach turned over even as her heart fluttered. She was an emotional disaster, something she'd never been. Probably because she'd never had strong feelings about any male, let alone one who needed things she couldn't give him. Because one thing was certain: she could never, *ever*, hurt Razr again. Nor could she watch it. Or even know it was happening.

She'd always thought she was strong, but the events of the day had proven that she was nothing of the sort.

"Jedda?"

She couldn't even look at him. Her shame had tied her in knots she wasn't sure would ever be untangled. "What?"

"I think we can kill Shrike."

Shame took a backseat to surprise, and she finally glanced up. Razr looked like hell, his expression bleak, his eyes haunted. Gods, she'd hurt him so badly, hadn't she? "What do you mean? How?"

"My powers are bound, but the Enoch gem's aren't. Through the bond we share, I can access it."

Her heart gave an excited thump. Her world might be shit right now, but this was good news. Shrike had cursed her to growing misery, and although she hadn't told Razr, she could feel the crushing pressure of it even now. The moment they'd come back to the earthly realm from the elven one, she'd experienced a painful squeezing sensation, one that made her skin feel like shrink-wrap. She could only imagine how much worse it would get over the course of the next couple weeks.

"What kind of power are we talking about?"

"A concussive blast that will blow apart any demon it touches, including fallen angels." He gestured toward the door. "We'll tell his buddies out there that we have what he wants and we're ready to go."

"They'll want proof."

"We have the crystal horn. That'll get us inside the castle."

As far as suicidal propositions went, this was a good one. "And afterward? Assuming we survive?"

"Then you come back here and resume your life. I'll return to Sheoul-gra and pretend to keep looking for the Gems of Enoch. No one has to know I found them. You and your sister will be safe."

It was how it had to be and she knew it. At least, it was how it had to be until she found a replacement gem or died trying.

But she couldn't let it end like this. She moved to him, and when he tried to step back, she persisted. "I know this is going to sound crazy, but I... I think I love you." His eyes flared wide, but she didn't regret her words. "Thank you for finding me. I'm so glad it was you."

Razr's gaze was tortured, but etched in his expression was something else. Something she wished she hadn't seen.

Love. He loved her too.

Very slowly, he reached out and cupped her cheek, his thumb smoothing away the teardrop rolling down her face and the tiny gem that formed behind it. She moaned as he lowered his mouth to hers and kissed her with so much tenderness and passion her knees nearly buckled. Heat spread through her veins, followed by a chill that sat on her skin like frost.

This was it. Good-bye.

When he pulled away, it was clear he knew it too.

# Chapter Fourteen

The journey to Shrike's place, mostly via Harrowgate with a little walking, was silent. Shrike's goons weren't the talkative type, for which Razr was enormously grateful. And Jedda...she just seemed broken.

Because of him. Because he'd made her hurt him and because there was no point in trying to earn her forgiveness or make her feel better. The angrier she was at him, the better.

But it sucked. More than having his wings bound by gold rope. More than being flogged on a regular basis. More than being kicked out of Heaven in disgrace.

On top of it all, he was going to lose her. She would eventually move on to a new male, maybe some hot fucking Legolas from Pandora. Or whatever.

*Fuck.*

He kept an eye on her as they approached the ballroom where Shrike was playing a game of darts. The dart board was unique, though: a demon's crucified body, with no discernible point system. Well, Razr would spot Shrike points for creativity, as well as a handicap for his mental disorder.

Ramreels with their unholy halberds stood like statues at evenly spaced intervals around the room, their piggy eyes watching Razr and Jedda's every move. They were big bastards, over seven feet tall with thick muscles under their fur. Or did they have wool? Razr had never asked, even though he'd encountered hundreds over the years. Ramreels were sort of all-purpose demons, common and plentiful enough to form armies but capable enough to act singly as bodyguards or even butlers. Apparently, they were even good cooks.

One thing they weren't, though, was subtle. Not when they resembled giant rams, carried halberds, and stomped their hooves on the floor in anticipation as they were doing now. They wanted to fight, and the tension in the room only fueled their bloodlust.

"We have what you want," Razr announced, getting right to it.

Shrike's lips peeled back from his straight, white teeth. Dude had a good dentist. "I knew you'd come through for me. Let me see."

Jedda had carried the horn in a black velvet bag to the castle, but now she gave it to Razr. She'd said she couldn't touch quartz crystal, but she hadn't said why. Doing so would have required more talking than she was apparently willing to do.

He reached into the bag and pulled out the heavy crystal sculpture.

"That wasn't easy to acquire," she said, following the script they'd worked out before leaving the apartment. Shrike needed to believe she'd found it and not that Razr had borrowed it from Azagoth.

Shrike's eyes, locked on the horn, glittered with greed. "That's why I hired you."

"Hired?" Fists clenched, she took a step toward him as if she wanted to throttle him. *That's my girl.* "Seriously? *Hired?* You gave me no choice. You forced me."

"Forced?" Shrike asked innocently. "Such an ugly word. I gave you *incentive.* But I don't go back on my word. I'll pay, of course."

"Yes," Razr said softly, "you will."

He moved toward the fallen angel as if to hand him the horn, but with every step he drew on the power of the Enoch gem, power that streamed from Jedda in a shaft of light that was blinding to him, but invisible and undetectable to everyone else. The energy building inside him churned and swelled, filling him with a unique ecstasy he'd not experienced for a century.

Battle lust scorched his veins, and anticipation made his fingers flex. He'd needed this for a long time. This was what he was born to do, and he had a lot of fury to unleash.

"Wait!" A familiar voice screeched from somewhere in the building. The sound of running footsteps pounded toward them.

Could it be...

A female in black leather pants and a silver crop-top burst into the great hall at the top of the grand staircase, her short chestnut hair curling around pierced ears Razr used to nibble.

He stumbled backward in shock, severing his link to Jedda. "*Darlah?*"

"Razriel?"

They stared at each other, and he wondered if she was as numb as he was.

"Darlah?" Jedda eased up beside him. "As in, *Darlah?* Your gem angel buddy? Your *lover?*"

"Ex-lover," he muttered. By the look on Shrike's face, the lover thing was news to him, and he wasn't happy about it.

"Someone had better explain what's happening," Shrike growled. "How do you know each other? Besides intimately."

Darlah, her face pale, didn't take her golden brown eyes off Razr as she descended the stairs. "Razriel was one of the Triad."

Suddenly, everything clicked into place. Razr's ex-lover was why Shrike had known about the *Azdai* glyph. He'd been meting out the punishment Darlah required. And she was also his source of information about the Gems of Enoch. But he hadn't known everything, which meant Darlah had been sparing with the details. She'd been smart to keep some things to herself, but Razr wouldn't expect anything else from her. He might have been the team leader and Ebel had been the brute force, but she'd been the strategist.

"Darlah, what are you doing here?" He gestured to Shrike. "With this crazy motherfucker."

Laughing bitterly, she stepped onto the landing. "Did you really think I'd go back to Heaven without my gem? Ebel found his and they still killed him. Imagine what they'd do to you or me."

"Bullshit," he snapped, angry at this betrayal. She'd been hiding all this time, and worse, she'd been hiding in a psychotic fallen angel's tacky lair. "Ebel is dead because his stone was tainted by evil, not because he returned to Heaven with it."

She cocked an eyebrow. "And how was he tainted by the evil?"

Razr threw up his hands in frustration. "Obviously, he must have bonded with the host. And because she was evil, he went insane and..." He trailed off, sickened by the implications of what he'd just voiced.

A glance at Jedda, at the trauma in her expression, confirmed his suspicion, and now it all made sense. Ebel's proximity to Manda and the evil taint of the stone had released evil in him, too. He must have raped her, sealing the malevolence in his soul. When he killed her and took the stone, the evil went with him, and he'd had to be destroyed.

How much of that had Jedda witnessed? No wonder she'd been terrified back in Azagoth's treasure room when she'd learned the Ice Diamond was his. She'd seen an angel behave in the most heinous of ways. And Razr's own behavior hadn't exactly been exemplary.

"It doesn't matter," Darlah said. "I'm not going back. But I do want my fucking stone." She snarled at Jedda. "I was close. So close. But your bitch of a sister had powerful friends."

Jedda sucked air. "You know who I am?"

"Fool," Darlah spat, her lips twisted in an ugly knot of rage. He used to kiss that mouth. Now he just wanted to gargle with kerosene to get the bad taste out of his own mouth. "That's why we chose you to find the gemstones. We figured you'd know where to find Reina."

"And if Jedda couldn't? Or wouldn't?" Razr shot back. "What then?"

Shrike tossed a dart, and it made a sickening squishy noise on impact with the dead demon's third eye. It really was an impressive shot, Razr supposed.

"We were hoping Jedda could find the bracelet as well as the matching gemstone." Shrike swung back around to Razr and Jedda. "But if not, we figured we could still get Jedda's."

"Jedda's is useless without my ring," Razr pointed out. "And you couldn't have known I'd randomly show up at the dinner party."

Darlah laughed. "I admit, that was a stroke of luck, but I would have found you eventually." She held up her arm to reveal her severed hand, making clear that she'd have done the same to him to get the ring.

Ah, shit. This situation could go bad, and fast, because clearly, they'd been prepared to kill Jedda to get the stone, and now they were prepared to kill or dismember him, as well. Wasn't going to happen, though. No way.

"Well," Shrike said with a dramatic sigh—because fallen angels were fucking drama queens, "I admit I'm kind of at a loss. I'm not sure where we go from here. I'm guessing you didn't bring Darlah's gem and bracelet."

"Even if we had," Jedda snapped, "do you think we'd give them to you now? You were planning to kill me, you bastard." She pegged Darlah with an accusing glare. "Bastards."

"Darlah," Razr warned, "you know Heaven is going to find out about this. They'll never let you back in."

"Good!" She threw out her arms and her bound wings popped from her back. They'd been beautiful once, white with shiny mink tips. Now they were trussed like a roast turkey, with thick gold rope strangling the feathers and bones. Razr's looked like that too, and seeing hers made them throb. "Let them find out. Let them sever my wings so I can have the power of the Fallen when they grow back. This is where I belong." She made an encompassing gesture. "This is where I will make my name. Here I can rule demons instead of serve angels."

"I've heard that story before," he said, as every tale of Satan's rebellion filtered through his mind. "It won't end well for you."

"No, my love," she whispered. "It won't end well for *you*."

Suddenly, a flash of light and a massive swell of scorching heat slammed into him, knocking him into a pillar twenty feet away. Jedda screamed as she careened off another pillar and into a wall with a sickening crunch. Another blast hit Razr before he could recover. Fire seared his skin, and the stench of singed hair filled his nostrils. Every muscle screamed in agony at the cellular level from the impact of the energy wave.

Only Shrike would have been capable of using that particular fallen angel weapon, and with Razr's power bound by angels, he couldn't fight it. He needed Jedda.

He reached out with his mind for the power of the Enoch gem... But there wasn't so much as a spark. What the hell?

Groaning, he rolled to his feet as Darlah heaved the blade of a sword down so close to his head that he felt the gentle kiss of it passing next to his ear. Sweeping his legs out, he caught her at the knees, bringing her down in a clumsy sprawl. But she was quick, and she was on her feet before he made it halfway to Jedda, who hadn't moved since the initial blast. Blood and gemstones formed in a puddle around her, expanding with alarming speed.

*Be okay. Please be okay—*

Something hit him from behind, knocking him to his knees with the force of the blow and the intensity of the pain. Warm blood splashed down his back and hips, and holy fucking shit, he might have lost an organ or two as well. As he hit the floor, realization clobbered him as hard as the blow had.

He'd taken a strike from a halberd, its sharp, foot-long head buried deep between his shoulder blades.

His ears rang, and he wasn't sure which was louder: his pounding pulse or Shrike's maniacal laughter. He was going to die like this. And so was Jedda, if he couldn't rouse her to consciousness.

Desperately, he dragged himself toward her, the halberd's heavy pole-handle scraping the floor and sending fresh rounds of agony clawing through him with every inch of progress he made.

Almost there...almost there... "Jedda," he rasped. Her eyes opened, dazed and lacking the brilliance he loved to see. "I need your power, baby. You can do it."

All around her, the ice-blue glow of the gem's power flickered to life. But "flickered" was the key word. Her power was fluctuating, weak, and they were in some serious trouble.

\* \* \* \*

Jedda wasn't afraid of dying. Especially not if dying meant Razr could return to Heaven and be reinstated as an angel and would no longer suffer the horrific torture he'd been subjected to for years.

But dying for any other reason was bullshit, and the sight of him trying to drag himself to her, a weapon impaled in his back, misery etched on his handsome face... It made her angry and heartbroken and dammit, her will to live was stronger than this.

Even as her mind rallied, her body failed. Gemstones formed all around her, large ones, powerful ones. She wasn't just bleeding; her organs were failing.

A smile twisted Shrike's lips as he threw out his hand, and a sizzling strike of lightning hit Razr in the neck. He tried to scream, but the only thing that came from his ruined throat was smoke.

"No," she croaked. "*No!*"

Gritting her teeth, she found one last surge of energy. One last chance to end this. With a shout of agony, she lunged at Razr, sliding through her own slippery blood. Somehow, her hand found his, her fingers closing around the glowing gemstone in his ring.

It was enough. As if she'd plugged them into an electrical socket, they both lit up with an ice-blue aura of energy.

"Stop them!" Darlah shouted. Frantic, Razr's bitch of an ex reached for the nearest weapon, a dart, and hurled it at Jedda. But, just like in the mines, her body sensed danger, her skin hardened into a diamond shield, and the dart bounced harmlessly to the floor.

Oh, that *necrocrotch skank* had to die. And if Jedda survived this, she was going to give Suzanne a huge high-five.

Shrike produced a ball of fire at his fingertips, but he wasn't fast enough. Razr, energized by the gem connection he shared with Jedda, triggered an atomic shockwave of death in an expanding circular wave. The entire building shook, and a chorus of screams filled the air. Blood and body parts rained down in a gruesome tempest of death, and when it was over, nothing was left standing.

Not even the necrocrotch skank.

Pain throbbed through every cell, but it was the exquisite pain of regeneration, and Jedda welcomed it. Groaning, she swept her arm through the gemstones on the floor, absorbing them back into her body to accelerate the process.

"Razr?" Weakly, she lifted her head, expecting to see him picking up his own pieces.

Instead, she saw him lying in a pool of blood, his eyes open and glazed with pain. Sure, the halberd impaled in his back probably had something to do with that, but worse, so did the fact that his damned *Azdai* glyph was lit up.

"Fucking angels." Emotion choked her, leaving her voice completely wrecked. "How can they do this to you? How?"

Tears streamed down her face, and the gems that formed from them clinked on the floor, creating a heart-wrenching score for what had turned out to be both a victory and a defeat. She'd survived, they'd *both* survived, but Razr's life hadn't changed.

Sobbing, she crawled over to him and wrenched the halberd from his body. He didn't make a sound, and for a moment afterward, she thought he was dead. Diamond dust poofed in a massive cloud as she gathered him in her arms, but when he took a deep, ragged breath, she cried out in relief.

"What can I do?" she asked. Begged, really. "I won't hurt you again. Anything but that."

Blood dripped from the corner of his mouth. "Stop," he wheezed. "Let it happen."

Let *what* happen? "I don't understand. Razr? Please..."

"Shh." His hand shook as he reached up and traced a finger over her lips. "You need...to go."

"No—"

"You..." He swallowed. "You said...you'd do anything. I want you to go."

"Why?"

"Angels." He shivered violently. "They're coming."

Terror turned her blood to ice. They'd kill her. They'd kill her to release the Enoch gem from storage. Panic threatened to swamp her, but before the diamond dust made another glittery show, she pulled it back. No. She would not give in to fear. And she would not give in to Razr.

If angels were coming, she'd stay.

One way or another, Razr's nightmare was coming to an end.

# Chapter Fifteen

Razr writhed as Jedda held him, her soft hands stroking his hair, the only place her touch didn't make him want to scream in pain. Why wouldn't she leave? They'd won the battle, which meant she was free. If she didn't get the fuck out of here she was going to get caught by whoever showed up to either kill him or torture the hell out of him, and, while he could accept his fate, there was no way he could allow harm to come to her.

They would *have* to kill him if they hurt her.

He wished he could see her, but Shrike's lightning strike had burned his eyes, and now everything was in fuzzy grayscale. Jedda's beautiful face was nothing more than a blob of haze.

"I hate this." She sniffled, and his heart ached. "I hate this so much. I hate angels for doing this to you!"

"We're not overly fond of you, either," came a deep voice.

Jedda jumped, sending a fresh wave of hellish pain and dread through Razr's body. "Who the hell are you?"

"My name is Gadreel."

Gadreel...Razr panted through another wave of misery as he ran the name through his weary brain. "Gadreel," he murmured. "Archangel?"

Jedda gasped. "You're an archangel?"

"Last time I looked."

"Can you do something about Razr? Can you stop his pain?"

Instantly, the agony melted from his body, and he sagged against Jedda in blessed relief. Relief he had a feeling would be short-lived.

At least his vision had cleared. He'd be able to see death coming.

Today, death was a big dude in black slacks, a black shirt, and a long black trench coat. Fitting, Razr supposed. All he was missing was an executioner's hood.

"You two made a mess." Gadreel looked around the castle ruins, his long blond hair blowing in the breeze from the gaping hole in the south wall. "And if I'm not mistaken, that decapitated head over there belongs to Darlah."

Razr struggled to sit up, his body feeling as weak as a newborn's. He blinked up at the newcomer. The angel looked familiar, but he couldn't figure out why. He'd have remembered meeting an archangel. Maybe he'd seen the guy in passing at some point. It wasn't as if every angel knew every other angel in Heaven, after all, and archangels were especially reclusive.

"I didn't expect you to be here so soon." Razr rolled his head to work out a kink in his neck. "My *Azdai* glyph just triggered."

"That isn't what drew me here." Gadreel pinned Jedda with his steely gaze. "The power of the Enoch gem did."

Razr inhaled a ragged breath as he shoved awkwardly to his feet. "Don't touch her," he growled. "Do *not* touch her."

"Why would I?"

Razr blinked in confusion. Did Gadreel not know that Jedda possessed the stone? "I don't understand."

Gadreel flared his gold-flecked white wings. "That's because you're a lesser angel." He sighed as if he felt sorry for those who weren't sitting at the top of the food chain like he was. The prick. "Your gem elf friend here is qualified to wield Gems of Enoch."

Jedda and Razr exchanged glances. Now Razr was really confused. "I thought only humans could do that."

"No, the rule is that demons and angels *can't*. Which means humans and elves *can*."

Relief nearly sapped Razr's energy right out of him. "Until I met Jedda I didn't even know elves existed."

"Few do," Gadreel said with a shrug. "They don't belong in our...reality, I guess you'd say. Their lives and deaths happen on another plane of existence. But because they are neutral forces, they can wield the Enoch gems as well as, or better than, any human."

Jedda stepped forward. "Mr., ah, Gadreel, can I ask why the

gems don't have exclusively 'good' vibes surrounding them? They're not even neutral. They're hard to pin down, really."

He inclined his head. "That's because each contains a small amount of demon blood."

Well, Razr hadn't seen that coming. "Why? Angel blood is far more powerful."

"Because the gems are used to fight demons. How would their energy know the difference between humans and demons without a baseline?" Gadreel's massive wings folded behind his back, the tips just barely kissing the floor. "Probably something we should have told you."

"Yeah. Probably." Razr couldn't keep the sarcasm out of his voice, and Gadreel shot him a glare. But hey, it could have been worse. A lot worse.

"Come on." Gadreel waved his hand, erasing the demon and fallen angel remains and sending their souls to Azagoth. The *griminions* would be disappointed to have their job stolen from them. "I'll zap the elf back to her realm and take you home."

Oh, fuck that. Razr took Jedda's hand and tugged her close, ignoring her little squeak of surprise. "I'm staying."

Gadreel wheeled around, his coat flapping at his calves. "What do you mean, you're staying?"

Razr took a deep breath and blurted, "I mean that I'm refusing reinstatement as an angel."

"What?" Jedda tugged on his hand. "Are you serious?"

"Yeah," he said, grinning. "I am."

The archangel stared. "No one refuses angelic reinstatement."

"Uh, dude." Razr couldn't believe Gadreel had said that. He knew of two angels who had refused in the last few years. "It's happened a lot recently. You guys are breaking rules left and right."

Gadreel flared his wings again, either out of boredom or irritation. Probably irritation. "Armageddon is nigh."

Okay, sure, as an angel battling demons, Razr had known that Armageddon would eventually come, and every fight had been considered preparation. Thanks to the Four Horsemen, it had almost happened. But, also thanks to the Horsemen—as well as a few angels and demons—it had been pre-empted. World saved. Humanity rescued. Whether that was a good thing or a bad one had yet to be seen.

"I hate to tell you this," Razr said as he bent to retrieve Azagoth's crystal horn, "but we just stopped Armageddon. We're cool now."

Gadreel's eyes glowed so bright that Razr and Jedda stepped back. "I'm talking about Satan. He's contained, but he'll be loose soon. We must prepare."

Jedda's breath caught, and she let out a strangled squeak. "How soon?"

"Nine hundred and ninety-ish years," Razr replied as he kicked aside the halberd that had nearly split him in half. "Give or take a couple of years."

She gave him a you've-got-to-be-kidding me look. "You're alarmed now by something that won't happen for almost a thousand years?"

"A thousand years is the blink of an eye for angels." Gadreel turned to Razr. "Now stop being a fool and come with me. The Archangel Council will want to see you."

Razr tucked the crystal horn in his pocket and stood his ground. "I'm staying here."

"Razr, no." Jedda drew him aside, keeping her voice low. "I can't watch you be tortured over and over. Not for me."

"Oh, for crying out loud," Gadreel snapped. "We can reinstate you as an angel and you won't have to live in Heaven." He cocked his head and drilled Razr with a look he could only describe as cruel. "But there's a catch. Naturally."

"Naturally," Razr muttered.

"Azagoth likes your work with the Memitim. You will live in Sheoul-gra and continue in his service except when you and Jedda are needed for battles with the Enoch gem. And you'll continue your search for the remaining gem and jewelry."

Razr's heart pounded against his ribs as both excitement and worry squeezed his chest. He didn't want to lie about Jedda's sister, but he'd promised to protect her, as well. "What happens when I find them?"

"Since we have the amethyst set, we'll assign it, and you'll form another Triad."

Jedda grinned. "We'll be like the Avengers."

Gadreel scowled. "The what?"

"Nothing," Razr said. "I agree. To everything."

"Wait." Jedda pulled Razr aside once again. "What if *I* don't agree?"

His heart stopped pounding. Just seized up like an engine. "What are you saying? That you don't want to be with me?"

"Of course I want to be with you." She licked her lips and cast a worried look at Gadreel. "But I need to know you want that too. I know you just said you did, but earlier, before the battle... It was good-bye, and you know it."

He pulled her into a tight embrace, sorry he'd put her through that. "I had to, Jedda. I was afraid for your life. I didn't want to lead anyone to you."

"So you really want me?"

"I've never wanted anything more."

Gadreel huffed. "I give up. Come to the Archangel Council on your own. You have forty-eight hours." He waved his hand, and ecstasy tore through Razr as his body filled with light.

His wings, once strangled by rope, burst from his back in a twenty-foot span of iridescent pearl, and power surged through his veins in a cascade of glorious heat. A zipper-like sensation skittered over his skin as the tattoos meant to add an extra layer of restraint on his angelic powers dematerialized.

He was free.

"Razr," Jedda whispered in awe as she fingered one silky feather and sent shivers of pleasure through his every nerve ending. "Your wings... They're beautiful."

"Razriel," Gadreel corrected her. Then he disappeared in a flash of light, leaving them alone in the wrecked castle.

"Call me whatever you want," Razr said as he pulled her against him. "I'll always answer."

He felt her smile against his chest, and it warmed him like nothing else ever had. "You have no choice now that we're bonded."

Gently, he pressed a kiss into her hair. "I had a choice," he reminded her. "I chose you."

# Chapter Sixteen

"Well, what do you think of our new home?"

So excited she could hardly contain the happy gemstone tears, Jedda looked around the manor Azagoth had chosen for them on the outskirts of his little city. The decor was exquisite in jewel tones and a mix of ancient Greece and modern London, complete with a MIND THE GAP sign hanging in the kitchen.

But it was the bedroom that had Jedda finally shedding a couple of tiny diamonds.

All of Razr's hideous burlap robes were gone, replaced by a closet full of new clothes. Even now, he looked absolutely edible in a pair of jeans, an untucked sapphire shirt...and flip-flops. Well, she couldn't fix everything.

Even better, a bed made to sleep four people comfortably took up half of the room, there was a hot tub in the corner—a gift from Zhubaal and his mate, Vex, both of whom seemed to have an affinity for them—and in another corner was a reading nook full of fiction and nonfiction books about elves and gemstones.

The most fascinating thing, though, was the item lying in the middle of the bed. The note attached to it said simply, *Enjoy ~ Azagoth.*

Razr scowled and picked it up. "Why would he give us a crystal dildo? You're like, allergic to quartz or something, right?"

Her cheeks burned so hot she thought she might catch on fire. "Not...exactly."

"You said you can't touch it."

"I said I can't touch it in public." She gave him a sheepish grin. "Or if I plan to get anything done."

He narrowed his eyes at her. "What are you not telling me?"

Emboldened by his curiosity, she slowly peeled out of her clothes, making him watch as he held the sex toy in a white-knuckled death grip. When she was completely naked, she gestured to him. "Your turn."

Cursing, he tossed the dildo on the bed and stripped out of his clothes so fast he might have set a record. He stood before her, his massive erection curving upward into his flat belly. Lust rolled off him in a wave of heat, and a rush of liquid desire dampened her core.

Not yet. First, she had to taste him.

She sauntered over, loving how his breath hitched as she went to her knees in front of him. When she looked up at him, her own breath caught at the worship in his expression. He wanted her as badly as she wanted him, and nothing had ever been such a turn-on.

Licking her lips, she gripped his shaft with one hand and cradled his sac with the other. He moaned when she closed her mouth over him and took him deep.

"Jedda..."

Desire curled in her gut at the sound of her name, spoken in a breathy, needy rasp. Sucking at the tip of his cock, she pumped her fist, drawing a pleasured hiss from him and a sigh of anticipation from her. His balls swelled as she rolled them between her fingers, and with each flick of her tongue on the underside of his shaft, he jerked and let out whispered curses.

She loved the power she had over him in this moment. She could do anything she wanted to him, and he'd beg her for it.

She eyed the dildo on the bed and...nah. Not now. But soon. They'd play with it, and he'd let her put it anywhere she wanted to.

"Don't...stop..." His guttural voice told her he was on the edge, was right there, and sure enough, he came with a roar, his hips bucking so hard she had to grip them to steady herself. He tasted like honey and sunshine, which was a seriously pleasant surprise after dating only human men.

Angels were pretty awesome, she decided.

She gave him a final lick, from the base of his shaft to the top, and then she climbed onto the bed, the dildo within reach. "So," she said saucily, "wanna see what happens when I touch quartz crystal?"

"Oh, yeah." Razr's half-lidded eyes took her in as she palmed the penis-sized dildo.

Instant ecstasy washed over her, and she moaned as the vibrations inherent to quartz filled her body. This was why gem elves avoided it...except in private. Contact in public could end in humiliation and sometimes, she'd heard, arrest.

Razr joined her on the mattress, and when he touched her, he too was swept up in the seismic eroticism.

"Ah...damn," he choked out. "This is like... It's like..."

"Like being held at the verge of orgasm," she finished hoarsely. "Just wait...until I show you...all the things...we can...do with...it." She tossed the dildo aside, needing to catch her breath, but more importantly, needing to be with *him*. There was time for toys and exploration later.

Panting, she pulled him to her and kissed him as he settled his heavy body on top of her.

"Be with me," she whispered.

"Always." He spread her legs and kissed his way down her neck, her breasts, her belly, nipping and licking, teasing her so brutally that she was trembling by the time he dipped his head and kissed her center.

"Yes," she moaned, but he denied her.

He nipped her inner thigh and then nuzzled her sex, his fingers feathering light strokes in the crease of her thigh. Desperate for more, she jammed her fingers through his hair and guided him where she needed him to be.

He chuckled softly, but he didn't spend any more time torturing her. Easing his fingers inward, he penetrated her with one as he flicked the tip of his tongue across her clit. She whimpered with need, bucking when he did it again.

Fiery lashes of pleasure whipped through her as he tongued her and pumped his fingers in her slick core, and with every second that passed, the fever inside her built.

"You taste like cinnamon." His voice was rough. So male. She loved it. "I'm going to have you for dessert every night."

On that promise, he replaced his fingers with his tongue, lapping at her hungrily, his masculine purr of need vibrating her from her core to her breasts, setting her off like an erotic bomb.

She panted through the detonation, the orgasm shattering her, emotionally and physically. She didn't even have a chance to recover before he mounted her, impaling her with his hard shaft and setting her off again.

He rocked against her, every stroke of his cock hitting a spot deep inside that kept her riding the wave of ecstasy that went on and on. How was this even possible? Her thoughts were a blur as he kissed her deeply and surged into her like they were riding waves in a stormy sea.

His wings erupted from his back and came down around them both, sealing them in a cocoon of safety and sensation. And as he shouted in his own climax, she joined him. Loudly. Breathlessly.

This was power. Not the kind that came from gemstones or spells or Heaven.

This power came from love, and it was the strongest of them all.

* * * *

Also from 1001 Dark Nights and Larissa Ione, discover Azagoth, Hades, and Z.

Sign up for the 1001 Dark Nights Newsletter
and be entered to win a Tiffany Key necklace.

There's a contest every month!

Go to www.1001DarkNights.com to subscribe.

As a bonus, all subscribers will receive a free
1001 Dark Nights story
The First Night
by Lexi Blake & M.J. Rose

Turn the page for a full list of the
1001 Dark Nights fabulous novellas...

# Discover 1001 Dark Nights Collection Four

*Go to www.1001DarkNights.com for more information.*

ROCK CHICK REAWAKENING by Kristen Ashley
A Rock Chick Novella

ADORING INK by Carrie Ann Ryan
A Montgomery Ink Novella

SWEET RIVALRY by K. Bromberg

SHADE'S LADY by Joanna Wylde
A Reapers MC Novella

RAZR by Larissa Ione
A Demonica Underworld Novella

ARRANGED by Lexi Blake
A Masters and Mercenaries Novella

TANGLED by Rebecca Zanetti
A Dark Protectors Novella

HOLD ME by J. Kenner
A Stark Ever After Novella

SOMEHOW, SOME WAY by Jennifer Probst
A Billionaire Builders Novella

TOO CLOSE TO CALL by Tessa Bailey
A Romancing the Clarksons Novella

HUNTED by Elisabeth Naughton
An Eternal Guardians Novella

EYES ON YOU by Laura Kaye
A Blasphemy Novella

BLADE by Alexandra Ivy/Laura Wright
A Bayou Heat Novella

DRAGON BURN by Donna Grant
A Dark Kings Novella

TRIPPED OUT by Lorelei James
A Blacktop Cowboys® Novella

STUD FINDER by Lauren Blakely

MIDNIGHT UNLEASHED by Lara Adrian
A Midnight Breed Novella

HALLOW BE THE HAUNT by Heather Graham
A Krewe of Hunters Novella

DIRTY FILTHY FIX by Laurelin Paige
A Fixed Novella

THE BED MATE by Kendall Ryan
A Room Mate Novella

NIGHT GAMES by CD Reiss
A Games Novella

NO RESERVATIONS by Kristen Proby
A Fusion Novella

DAWN OF SURRENDER by Liliana Hart
A MacKenzie Family Novella

# Discover 1001 Dark Nights Collection One

*Go to www.1001DarkNights.com for more information.*

# Discover 1001 Dark Nights Collection Two

*Go to www.1001DarkNights.com for more information.*

# Discover 1001 Dark Nights Collection Three

*Go to www.1001DarkNights.com for more information.*

# About Larissa Ione

Air Force veteran Larissa Ione traded in a career as a meteorologist to pursue her passion of writing. She has since published dozens of books, hit several bestseller lists, including the New York Times and USA Today, and has been nominated for a RITA award. She now spends her days in pajamas with her computer, strong coffee, and fictional worlds. She believes in celebrating everything, and would never be caught without a bottle of Champagne chilling in the fridge…just in case. After a dozen moves all over the country with her now-retired U.S. Coast Guard spouse, she is now settled in Wisconsin with her husband, her teenage son, a rescue cat named Vegas, and her very own hellhound, a King Shepherd named Hexe.

For more information about Larissa, visit www.larissaione.com.

# Discover More Larissa Ione

*Azagoth: A Demonica Underword Novella* by Larissa Ione, Now Available

Even in the fathomless depths of the underworld and the bleak chambers of a damaged heart, the bonds of love can heal...or destroy.

He holds the ability to annihilate souls in the palm of his hand. He commands the respect of the most dangerous of demons and the most powerful of angels. He can seduce and dominate any female he wants with a mere look. But for all Azagoth's power, he's bound by shackles of his own making, and only an angel with a secret holds the key to his release.

She's an angel with the extraordinary ability to travel through time and space. An angel with a tormented past she can't escape. And when Lilliana is sent to Azagoth's underworld realm, she finds that her past isn't all she can't escape. For the irresistibly sexy fallen angel known as Azagoth is also known as the Grim Reaper, and when he claims a soul, it's forever...

\* \* \* \*

*Hades: A Demonica Underworld Novella* by Larissa Ione, Now Available

A fallen angel with a mean streak and a Mohawk, Hades has spent thousands of years serving as Jailor of the Underworld. The souls he guards are as evil as they come, but few dare to cross him. All of that changes when a sexy fallen angel infiltrates his prison and unintentionally starts a riot. It's easy enough to quell an uprising, but for the first time, Hades is torn between delivering justice — or bestowing mercy — on the beautiful female who could be his salvation...or his undoing.

Thanks to her unwitting participation in another angel's plot to start Armageddon, Cataclysm was kicked out of Heaven and is now a fallen angel in service of Hades's boss, Azagoth. All she wants is to redeem herself and get back where she belongs. But when she gets trapped in Hades's prison domain with only the cocky but irresistible Hades to help her, Cat finds that where she belongs might be in the place she least expected…

* * * *

*Z: A Demonica Underworld Novella* by Larissa Ione, Now Available

Zhubaal, fallen angel assistant to the Grim Reaper, has spent decades searching for the angel he loved and lost nearly a century ago. Not even her death can keep him from trying to find her, not when he knows she's been given a second chance at life in a new body. But as time passes, he's losing hope, and he wonders how much longer he can hold to the oath he swore to her so long ago…

As an *emim*, the wingless offspring of two fallen angels, Vex has always felt like a second-class citizen. But if she manages to secure a deal with the Grim Reaper — by any means necessary — she will have earned her place in the world. The only obstacle in the way of her plan is a sexy hardass called Z, who seems determined to thwart her at every turn. Soon it becomes clear that they have a powerful connection rooted in the past…but can any vow stand the test of time?

# On behalf of 1001 Dark Nights,
Liz Berry and M.J. Rose would like to thank ~

Steve Berry
Doug Scofield
Kim Guidroz
Jillian Stein
InkSlinger PR
Dan Slater
Asha Hossain
Chris Graham
Pamela Jamison
Fedora Chen
Jessica Johns
Dylan Stockton
Richard Blake
BookTrib After Dark
and Simon Lipskar

CPSIA information can be obtained
at www.ICGtesting.com
Printed in the USA
FSHW022043271118
54084FS

9 781945 920219